LEAVING HOME

"I know, I know. The Interlochen School happens to be heaven on earth," Jessica said, mimicking Elizabeth. "But it also happens to be heaven on the other *side* of the earth!"

Elizabeth shook her head. "You don't understand," she said flatly. "It's Switzerland. I can't really explain why I feel the way I do, but I just know I have to go there. And the Interlochen School would be the most marvelous place in the world to study creative writing!"

Jessica gave her twin an alarmed glance. She didn't like the sound of this—not one little bit. It sounded positively dangerous. The very best thing would be to nip the whole idea in the bud *before* Elizabeth started getting too serious about living in Switzerland for a year!

Bantam Books in the Sweet Valley High Series
Ask your bookseller for the books you have missed

SWEET VALLEY HIGH

LEAVING HOME

Written by
Kate William

Created by
FRANCINE PASCAL

BANTAM BOOKS
TORONTO • NEW YORK • LONDON • SYDNEY • AUCKLAND

RL 6, IL age 12 and up

LEAVING HOME
A Bantam Book / August 1987
2nd printing . . . March 1988

Sweet Valley High is a trademark of Francine Pascal

Conceived by Francine Pascal

Produced by Cloverdale Press, Inc.
133 Fifth Avenue, New York, NY 10003

Cover art by James Mathewuse

ISBN 0-553-27631-X

Published simultaneously in the United States and Canada

Bantam Books are published by Bantam Books, a division of Bantam Doubleday
Dell Publishing Group, Inc. Its trademark, consisting of the words "Bantam
Books" and the portrayal of a rooster, is Registered in U.S. Patent and
Trademark Office and in other countries. Marca Registrada. Bantam Books,
666 Fifth Avenue, New York, New York 10103.

PRINTED IN THE UNITED STATES OF AMERICA

O   11 10 9 8 7 6 5 4 3 2

LEAVING HOME

One

Jessica Wakefield could barely contain her excitement. "Look, you guys," she hissed, peering through a pair of new binoculars that she had borrowed from Randy Lloyd, her latest admirer. "Do you see that surfer out there in the water? The big blond with huge muscles?"

Enid Rollins and Jessica's twin sister, Elizabeth, exchanged amused glances. It was late in the afternoon, and the three girls were sitting on the beach, enjoying the Southern California sunshine and catching up on the latest gossip. Or at least Elizabeth and Enid were *trying* to catch up. Jessica was making conversation practically impossible. Anytime Enid or Elizabeth started talking, she interrupted them as she spotted another gorgeous surfer.

1

"Do you think Randy knew you were going to put his present to this kind of use?" Enid asked, her green eyes twinkling.

Jessica frowned, still peering out at the shoreline. "Of course not," she said. "But I don't care what Randy thinks. He's too—she shrugged, searching for the right word—"too *boring*," she said at last, flipping her silky blond hair back with one hand.

But Jessica knew that Enid Rollins would never understand. How could she, when she herself was completely and utterly predictable? Jessica couldn't believe her twin had chosen Enid for her best friend. She sighed and set her binoculars down. It wasn't as if Jessica hadn't done her best to point out Enid's shortcomings to her sister, either. Elizabeth just refused to listen, insisting Enid was loyal, dependable, and trustworthy—traits she valued most in a best friend. Jessica wrinkled her nose at the thought. Loyal, dependable, and trustworthy—it sounded like a motto for the Girl Scouts, not a way to describe anyone worth getting to know!

But then there was no explaining differences in taste. And when it came to differences, Jessica and Elizabeth were experts! Not that anyone would ever guess to look at them that they could disagree about anything. Sixteen years old, the twins were model slim, with sunstreaked, shoulder-length blond hair and sparkling blue-green eyes fringed with dark lashes. Each girl had a tiny dimple that could be seen when she smiled. The resemblance between them was so strong that even their closest friends sometimes confused them.

But no one could ever confuse their behavior or attitudes. Elizabeth, who was four minutes older than Jessica, liked to take a big sister role, often advising or admonishing her impetuous twin. Most of the time Elizabeth's advice was sensible. That was partly because Elizabeth thought things through—she looked, as she liked to put it, while Jessica leaped. Elizabeth liked taking things steadily and slowly. She was deeply loyal to her best friend, Enid, and her boyfriend, Jeffrey French, and once she took an interest in something—such as writing for the school paper, *The Oracle*—she gave it her all.

Jessica loved her sister more than anything in the world and secretly admired her diligence and responsibility. But she couldn't help teasing her now and then for taking life so seriously. Jessica's rule was to live for the moment. Why commit herself to one boy when there was a whole beachful of gorgeous surfers to look at—and flirt with? And why spend hours working on homework when she could be working out with the cheerleading squad or shopping at the mall?

"I think Randy is cute," Enid objected, running a comb through her soft brown hair. "He's nice, Jessica. And he really cares about you."

Jessica could tell there was a reproach in Enid's words, but she decided to ignore it. "He *is* nice," she agreed lightly, picking up the binoculars again. Randy was a senior whom Jessica had dated a couple of times over the course of the past several weeks. "And," she added with a giggle, "he owns expensive binoculars. If he keeps lending me things, who knows how long I'll stay interested?"

"You're awful," Elizabeth scolded her twin. But her voice sounded slightly distracted. She had a large, colorful brochure open on her lap, and it was apparent that whatever she was reading had most of her attention.

"Wow," Jessica said, scanning the horizon again. "This is really terrific. I mean, look at this place! A beach—palm trees—gorgeous guys—the mountains just a couple of hours away. Who could ask for anything more than Sweet Valley?"

Enid put her comb back in her beach bag. "How about your twin, for starters?" she asked dryly. "Or haven't you noticed that Liz is half-way to Switzerland even as we speak?"

Jessica took the binoculars away from her face and fixed her sister with a piercing, blue-green gaze. "Liz, put that brochure away," she commanded, suddenly realizing what it was that

4

Elizabeth was so intent on. "I thought we were through with this Switzerland business!"

Elizabeth looked injured. "Come on, Jess. Switzerland happens to be a fascinating country. Regina Morrow says its incredibly beautiful. Up in the Alps, she says—"

"Stop!" Jessica shrieked, covering her ears with her hands. She looked at her sister with an expression of agony.

"How many times do we have to hear about what Regina Morrow has to say about Switzerland?" she demanded.

Regina Morrow was in the junior class at Sweet Valley High, along with Jessica, Elizabeth, and Enid. A startlingly beautiful girl, Regina was the only daughter of one of the wealthiest men in the valley. Her mother had been a fashion model, and Regina had been chosen to appear on the cover of *Ingenue* magazine once herself. But Regina had been born with a birth defect that left her hearing severely impaired. In the middle of her junior year she was sent to Switzerland for a series of treatments which gave her almost normal hearing ability.

For Regina, the long months in Switzerland had been lonesome and difficult. She had been separated from her family—and from Bruce Patman, her boyfriend. And she had to spend most of her time *in* the hospital, anxiously awaiting results from her treatments.

But even under those circumstances, Regina had fallen in love with the beautiful, mountainous country that had been her home. She sent postcards home describing the breathtaking views of the Alps, the crystal-blue lakes, and the warmth of the charming Swiss people. Elizabeth, whose imagination was easily fired, had decided long before that Switzerland had to be the most enchanting, romantic place on earth. She vowed to go one day. Lately Regina had received some letters from the friends she had made in Switzerland. And when she heard of these, Elizabeth was reminded of her earlier interest in going abroad.

And at about the same time Mr. Collins, her favorite teacher, suggested that Elizabeth read F. Scott Fitzgerald's *Tender Is the Night* for an extra-credit assignment. Suddenly Dick Diver, the protagonist of the novel, became Elizabeth's hero. She couldn't put the book down, and when she was finished with it, she had romanticized everything to do with Dick Diver—including Geneva, the city where he'd studied medicine. Now Switzerland seemed doubly charming to Elizabeth, and a few suggestions from Regina had actually led her to look into several programs that would allow her to have her senior year abroad in Switzerland. One, at the Interlochen School, actually offered several kinds of scholarship programs for American high school students. Elizabeth had thought and spoken of little but Switzerland and the Interlochen School since the brochure had arrived the previous week.

"Come on, you two. Just look at this," Elizabeth urged, spreading the brochure from the Interlochen School out on her striped beach towel. A magnificent scene of the Alps covered the front of the brochure, the picturesque school was nestled beside a sparkling blue lake under a stand of fir trees.

It really was beautiful, but Jessica had no intention of supporting her sister's enthusiasm. There was no way Jessica was going to let her twin take off and leave her!

For once, Enid and Jessica seemed to feel the same way. "You're really serious about this place, aren't you?" Enid asked anxiously, looking at the brochure over her friend's shoulder.

Elizabeth nodded, her eyes shining. "Now it's just a question of waiting to hear from Mr. Hummel, the headmaster." She sighed. "It's probably out of the question—I bet I'm too late to apply for a scholarship for next year." She pointed to a paragraph on the second page of the brochure. "See, they have a special creative-writing program that starts in the summer and lasts for all of the senior year." She stared dreamily out over the water. "Can you imagine taking creative-writing classes while looking out at the Alps for inspiration?" She shivered. "I think it would be the most wonderful thing in the whole world."

Enid frowned. "I don't want to sound selfish, but I hope this Mr. Himmel says it's too late. I couldn't stand the thought of you going so far away for so long!"

"It's Mr. Hummel, not Mr. Himmel," Elizabeth corrected her. "And it wouldn't be that long, Enid. Not when you consider that it's an opportunity to really live and write in Europe!" Looking starry-eyed, she sighed. "I keep telling myself not to get excited when the whole thing seems so unlikely. But I can't help it."

Jessica looked glum. "I thought twins were supposed to be close," she complained. "Haven't you always said how important it is for us to spend time together, Liz? I'd like to know how much time we're going to get to spend together when you're off somewhere wearing lederhosen and yodeling and chasing goats."

Elizabeth giggled. She couldn't believe how morose her sister looked. "You make it sound ridiculous, Jess. The Interlochen School happens to be internationally renowned. In fact—"

"I know, I know," Jessica said, cutting her off. "The Interlochen School happens to be heaven on earth." She mimicked her sister's tone and sniffed. "But it also happens to be heaven on the other *side* of the earth! Couldn't

8

you find someplace a little less remote if you're so bent on spending a year in boarding school?"

Elizabeth shook her head, her blond ponytail bobbing emphatically. "You don't understand," she said flatly. "It isn't the boarding-school part that matters." Her eyes shone. "It's Switzerland. I can't really explain why I feel the way I do, but I just know I have to go there." She hugged herself. "And I know the Interlochen School would be the most marvelous place in the world to study creative writing!"

Jessica gave her twin an alarmed glance. She didn't like the sound of this—not one little bit. It sounded positively dangerous. And, Jessica decided, the very best thing would be to nip the whole idea in the bud *before* Elizabeth started getting too serious about living in Switzerland for a year!

That night the twins and their parents drove twenty-five miles north of Sweet Valley to San Farando, a tiny town midway between their home and the state college, where the twins' older brother, Steven, was a freshman. The Wakefield family sometimes met there during the term when Steven was too busy to get home. The Wakefields loved San Farando, with its awesome views of the mountains, and they were especially fond of a small Mexican restaurant there called Pedro's. By seven-thirty all five

Wakefields were seated around a table, platters of steaming Mexican food before them.

"This looks a lot better than the food back at the dorm," Steven said, pushing back his dark hair and grinning. With his cheerful dark eyes and athletic build, Steven at eighteen bore a strong resemblance to Ned Wakefield, the twins' father.

"You won't be able to eat Mexican food in Switzerland," Jessica reminded her sister, popping a nacho into her mouth.

Steven raised his eyebrows. "Still Switzerland?" he inquired. "I was sure you'd have given up by now, Liz, and decided that the good old U.S.A. isn't that bad after all."

Elizabeth took a sip of water. As much as she adored her family, there were times when she didn't really understand them. Why couldn't they understand how important Switzerland was to her?

"Don't tease your sister, you two," Alice Wakefield said gently, her blue eyes showing concern. A successful interior designer, the twins' mother looked so young that she was often mistaken for their older sister.

Jessica put her fork down, her appetite fading. She wished her parents would *do* something about Elizabeth's crazy new plan. Why were they being so calm about it? Couldn't they see that this was really a life-and-death situation?

"Europe has really had it, anyway," Jessica

announced. "It's completely decaying over there, Liz. Why would you want to go sit around in some chalet when you could be right here on the beach, keeping up your tan?"

Elizabeth shook her head. "Don't you remember how wonderful it was when we went to France during spring vacation? You loved it! Besides, generation after generation of artists and writers have gone to Europe to soak up culture so they could perfect their visions." Her eyes widened dreamily. "And if Mr. Hummel lets me apply for a scholarship, I could go, too!"

"I think your vision isn't the only thing that needs perfecting," Steven grumbled. "It sounds to me as if your whole thought processes need a little reorganization."

Elizabeth frowned. "You aren't being fair. If I get in—"

"I think," Mr. Wakefield said, his tone clearly meant to put a stop to their bickering, "that all of this is contingent upon too many 'ifs' right now. Why don't we wait until we have a little more information before we get so excited about the whole thing?"

Jessica bit her lip. She knew that further discussion at that point was out of the question. But she also thought her father was wrong.

She knew her twin well enough to believe that it was too late to warn her about not getting excited. When Elizabeth decided she wanted something, she went after it and got it. And it looked as if Elizabeth had decided what she wanted.

Jessica was convinced now that they really had an emergency on their hands. She just couldn't believe her parents could stay so calm in the middle of a crisis.

Two

"I agree with you, Elizabeth," Maria Santelli declared, taking a spoonful of yogurt. "I think boarding school in Europe sounds incredible." Her brown eyes shone. "It sounds like something right out of a novel!"

The twins were eating lunch at one of the tables on the patio outside of Sweet Valley High with a small group of friends—Maria Santelli, a pert, pretty brunette who was on the cheerleading squad with Jessica; Winston Egbert, Maria's boyfriend; Lila Fowler, one of Jessica's closest friends; Enid; and Jeffrey French. Jeffrey looked glum when the conversation turned to Switzerland, but Elizabeth didn't seem to notice.

"If only it weren't so expensive." Elizabeth said, taking a tuna sandwich out of the bag she had brought from home.

Lila gave her a condescending smile. The only daughter of one of the wealthiest computer magnates in Southern California, Lila didn't know what the words "too expensive" meant. "Too bad we can't start a Fowler fund for travel abroad," she mused. "I'm sure my daddy could just deduct it. And it would be so *generous* of us."

Winston, a tall, lanky boy whose quick sense of humor had won him the reputation of class clown, looked up at Elizabeth with a grin. "Don't worry, Liz. I'll start an Egbert fund for travel abroad—and I don't even care whether it's deductible or not!"

Lila rolled her eyes. "Of course not. Nothing deducted from nothing comes out—nothing! Where would *you* get the money to send Liz to Switzerland?"

Winston pretended to look grieved. "She clearly knows nothing of my hidden resources," he said, holding his heart with mock pain. "Haven't you heard the news, Lila? I'm about to become filthy rich."

Maria giggled. "That's right. Winston's ship is about to come in. He's going to start showering me with expensive presents."

"Or at least pay for my half of the movies," Winston said generously, patting Maria's hand.

"Don't keep us in suspense, Winston," Lila said, looking temporarily interested. "Do you

14

have some rich relative who's deathly ill or something?"

"Nice thought, Lila," Winston said cheerfully. "I hate to disappoint you, but all my relatives are perfectly healthy." He grinned and flourished a small green ticket. "This is it, guys—the ticket to my success!"

Lila wrinkled her nose, turning back to her salad. "It's just a dumb lottery ticket," she complained.

"Did you hear that?" Winston demanded. "*Just* a lottery ticket, she says." He waved the ticket triumphantly. "It just so happens that my father bought me this ticket. And my father is an astonishingly lucky guy. He managed to get me for a son, right?"

"I'm sure he thanks his lucky star every day," Lila said sarcastically.

Jessica giggled. "Is your dad going to demand a cut if you win?" she asked.

Winston held the ticket up to the light. "Please," he said, shaking his head at her, "we're way too refined for that sort of arrangement, Jessica. When I win, I'm going to make sure everybody benefits! And the very first thing I'll do is send Liz to boarding school."

Jeffrey groaned, and everyone else laughed. Elizabeth leaned across the table to pluck the ticket from Winston's hand. "You're sweet, but I'm afraid the odds are against us," she said. She looked hard at the lottery ticket. If only

15

something like that really could do the trick! But she knew Winston would never win. No, the only thing to do was to hope that there was still time left to apply for a scholarship. Otherwise Switzerland was going to be completely out of the question.

Elizabeth suddenly noticed that the first three numbers on Winston's ticket were the same as Jeffrey's birthday: 712. Jeffrey's birthday was July 12. She patted his knee under the table with her left hand as she passed the ticket back to Winston. Jeffrey was being so quiet. She hoped he wasn't upset about anything.

"Now, listen, you guys," Winston said, carefully putting the ticket away inside his wallet. "I want you all to come over to my house tonight for a Get Rich Quick party. The lottery drawing is at ten o'clock, so make sure you're there in plenty of time." He grinned. "I don't want you to miss a single minute of my newfound wealth."

"Winston," Lila groaned. Lila didn't find wealth one bit amusing, and she clearly didn't appreciate Winston's jokes.

"You come, too, Lila," Winston said magnanimously. "I want you to be there so you can coach me on how to behave once I'm rolling in dough."

Maria giggled. "I can't wait till you're rich, Winston," she said. "Once you've won the lottery, will you start buying your own lunches?"

Everyone at the table laughed. Winston was fairly thin, but he was famous for his huge appetite. Once he had even tried to set the world record for pizza eating. And Maria had been contributing a good part of her allowance each week to keeping him full.

"I don't think it's so farfetched," Jessica objected. "I saw this guy on the news last week who won the lottery. He bought wonderful presents for all his friends," she added significantly.

"My intention exactly," Winston declared. "I'm serious," he added. "I want you all to come over tonight, OK?"

"You can count on it," Enid promised. "We wouldn't miss this for the world!"

Everyone else agreed. "This should be good," Lila declared, tossing back her auburn hair.

"Can we bring anything?" Elizabeth asked him.

Winston looked pained. "Are you kidding? This is the first party I'm throwing as a rich man, Liz." He laughed. "It's on me. And you can count on one thing. From now on, Winston Egbert is going to do things with style!"

Elizabeth and Jeffrey had made plans to meet after school and drive to the mall, where Jeffrey wanted to find a birthday present for his mother. Ordinarily Elizabeth loved shopping for gifts, but that afternoon her mind was only partly occupied by the search for the perfect present for Mrs. French. She kept wondering whether or not there would be a letter from Mr. Hummel and the Interlochen School waiting for her at home.

"I wish *I'd* win the lottery," Jeffrey said thoughtfully, leaning over a case in North's Jewelry Store and inspecting a display of watches. "My mom really wants a new watch, but these all look really expensive."

Elizabeth smiled. "Just wait," she said. "If I get to go to Switzerland, I'll be able to find gorgeous watches—for a fraction of what they cost here."

Jeffrey frowned, but he didn't say anything. "Let's get out of here," he said a minute later.

Elizabeth stopped by a small case near the doorway. "Look at that pin," she murmured, her eyes bright. It was the prettiest thing she had ever seen—a tiny circle of pearls. Elizabeth didn't usually notice jewelry, but she thought the pin was exquisite.

"It is pretty," Jeffrey said, putting his arm around her. "It would look really nice on you."

Elizabeth was thoughtful as they left the store together. "Jeffrey, you seem kind of quiet," she remarked as they made their way through the mall toward the last store Jeffrey wanted to look in. "Is anything wrong?"

Jeffrey looked at her, a funny expression on his face. "I guess—I don't know. It just gives me a really weird feeling to hear you talking about Switzerland. Liz, you're really serious about going, aren't you?"

Elizabeth stared at him. "Of course I'm serious!" she exclaimed. "Jeffrey, can you imagine how wonderful it would be for me to get a chance to study in Europe? I'd get to travel—to meet people. . . ." Her face flushed with excitement. "I think it would be the most wonderful thing in the entire world!"

"That's what I was afraid of," Jeffrey said softly. "Liz, I know I sound selfish, but I don't want you to leave." He frowned. "I don't even want you to *want* to leave, if that makes any sense."

Elizabeth smiled and patted his arm. "It does," she assured him. "I think it'd be strange if you didn't feel that way—at least a little." She tucked her arm through his. "It's only natural. But it's not like we couldn't stay in touch. There'd be vacations, and we could always write and everything." She smiled up at him affectionately. "And it wouldn't be for that long. Only for our senior year."

" 'Only for our senior year,' " Jeffrey repeated, shaking his head. "That's pretty funny, Liz! Especially coming from you—after all you and Todd went through when he moved to Vermont. Aren't you afraid the distance would get to be too much for us, too?"

Elizabeth shook her head impatiently. "Of course not! That was a completely different thing," she declared. She really didn't see how Jeffrey could think the separation would hurt them as a couple. What he said about her former boyfriend, Todd Wilkins, was true. But then, Elizabeth reasoned, Todd had moved away forever. Elizabeth knew that after her year abroad she would be coming back to Sweet Valley. She was convinced the separation wouldn't have the same impact on Jeffrey and her.

Besides, she didn't want to think back to the pain she had suffered when Todd had moved away. She was too busy looking at the display in the window of The Ski Shop. Imagine shussing down Mont Blanc or the Matterhorn! She could barely believe that in just a matter of months she might actually be living in Switzerland. It made her tingle all over just thinking about it.

It was hard to know how seriously to take Jeffrey's objections. Elizabeth knew she couldn't discount the risks of long-distance romance. After all, she *had* experienced the agonies of that firsthand. When Todd had had to move to Vermont, they had both been devastated. For a long time they had tried to keep their relationship going, but they eventually realized that it was too difficult. It seemed more important to go on living their lives—separately—however hard it had been at first.

So it wasn't as though Elizabeth didn't recognize how tough it was to carry on a long-distance relationship. And Switzerland was a lot farther

away than Vermont. Phone calls would be difficult, if not impossible; letters would take days
to get across the ocean. Everything back home
would seem very far away.

But Elizabeth couldn't make herself dwell on
those aspects of her year abroad. After all, she
and Jeffrey loved and trusted each other. They
had a strong relationship. Why couldn't they
sustain it?

And they had always been careful not to be
possessive of each other, or to limit each other's
activities in any way. They both believed that
each of them ought to keep trying as hard as
possible to meet new people and have new
experiences.

Elizabeth was certain that deep down Jeffrey
really felt the same way she did about the
Interlochen School. She was sure he really
wanted what was best for her. It occurred to
her that she might have made a mistake by not
emphasizing how much the year abroad meant
to her. From then on she would be sure to talk
about the school and the writing program much
more often. She could show Jeffrey all the brochures she had received and emphasize how
much the program meant to her.

That way he would realize how important it
all was, and he wouldn't feel left out of her
decision.

Elizabeth was certain that would be the best
way to handle it. And once he realized how

much—how *completely*—she wanted to go, she knew he would start to want it for her as well.

"Jeffrey, let's go back over to my house after we find something for your mom," she said impulsively. "I want to show you the book on Switzerland that I took out of the library yesterday."

Jeffrey's face was tense. "OK," he said briefly, looking away from her.

But Elizabeth was too busy studying The Ski Shop display to notice his expression. She could hardly wait to show him the chapter on famous writers' reactions to the Alps. Before long Jeffrey was going to be as excited as she was about studying abroad. She was absolutely sure of it!

Three

Winston and Maria were deep in conversation as they entered Drake's, a small convenience store downtown. It was late afternoon and they wanted to pick up some things for the Get Rich Quick party at Winston's that evening.

"How many of us will there be?" Maria asked as they walked down the aisle where the potato chips and soda were. "Let's see: the twins, Jeffrey, Lila, you and me—anybody else?"

"Enid," Winston reminded her. "And I ran into Regina Morrow and Bruce Patman before seventh period and asked them to come, too. Regina's brother Nicholas. Let's see who else. Oh, I asked Olivia and Roger." Roger Patman was Bruce's cousin, and Olivia was his girlfriend.

Maria giggled. "If you don't win the lottery,

23

maybe a few of your guests can make it up to you by giving you part of their allowances this week."

Winston laughed, too. Bruce Patman came from a family as wealthy as the Fowlers. In fact, the Patmans and Fowlers had been rivals for many years, often locking horns on community issues when one family wanted to prove it was more powerful than the other. "The Morrows aren't exactly on skid row, either," he reminded Maria. "I heard Regina's mother wants to buy her a Corvette for her birthday."

Maria shook her head in disbelief. "I can't even imagine living that way," she said, picking up a bag of potato chips and putting it in their basket. "Honestly, Winston—all kidding aside about this lottery business—I'm really glad you're as ordinary as I am when it comes to money. I think it would be a little creepy being able to buy anything you wanted."

Winston pretended to look grieved. "Does that mean we can't buy any cheese puffs?" he demanded.

Soon the two had burst out laughing. They pretended to fight over whether to buy pretzels or taco-flavored chips. Maria was just reaching down for a six-pack of root beer when she accidentally bumped into a lovely little girl, who looked about seven years old. The girl was holding up a big bag of cookies and looking all around

with a confused expression on her face. "Grandpa?" she said, her eyes big.

Just then an elderly man came around the
corner. "I'm right here, Lisa," he said, coming
over to the little girl and putting his arm around
her.

"Grandpa, can we get these?" the child asked
eagerly. "They're my favorite kind."

The old man looked upset as he patted his
granddaughter on the head. "Sweetheart, I told
you," he said in a low voice, "I'm trying not to
spend so much money on that stuff." He leaned
over to scoop her up in his arms. "But you can
have a big hug from Grandpa. How's that?" he
asked, rumpling her hair.

"Wow," Maria said under her breath as they
watched the old man take his granddaughter
up to the cash register. "See what I mean, Winston? It's so unfair! That man can't even afford
to buy his granddaughter a bag of cookies."

"Well," Winston said philosophically, "he can't
be *too* poor, or he wouldn't be shopping in
Drake's."

"That isn't true," Maria protested. "He looks
poor. His shoes are kind of shabby. And he's
only buying a carton of milk."

Winston followed her gaze. Maria was right.
The old man was neatly dressed, but his trousers were worn thin at the knees and slightly
frayed at the hems. He was carrying a navy
blue jacket, which looked a lot like the jacket

Winston had on, but his sweater was all stretched out and looked worn. The little girl, though perfectly groomed, was wearing a cotton dress that appeared to have been refitted for her—the hem had obviously been let down several times.

"Well," Winston said again, clearing his throat. Watching the old man and his granddaughter had made him feel really sad, but he didn't know what to say or do about it. It was warm in the store, and he took his jacket off. "Let's pay for this stuff and go back to my house," he suggested, going up to the register. The old man was just taking a five-dollar bill out of his wallet.

Winston and Maria heaped their purchases up on the counter and waited patiently as the old man put away his change. Setting his jacket down next to the root beer, Winston turned to resume his conversation with Maria. "Oh—I forgot the peanuts!" he exclaimed. He hurried back to the first aisle and chose the largest can he could find. By the time he got back to the register, the old man and his granddaughter had gone.

"What's wrong?" Maria asked several minutes later. They were out in the parking lot, and Winston, who had just finished loading the food into the backseat of his family's station wagon, was frowning at the jacket in his hands.

"I think that guy took my jacket," he muttered, slipping the navy blue coat on. Sure enough, it was a couple of sizes larger than Winston's—and much older. It felt as if it had been worn for years.

"You're kidding," Maria said. "You mean he took yours by mistake?"

"He must've confused them. I set mine down on top of the root beer, and—" Winston broke off. "Oh, well, I'll just go in and leave my phone number with the guy at the register. I'm sure the old man will realize his mistake the second he tries to put my jacket on—it'll be too small for him. Then he can call me and we'll swap them.

"I'll wait out here for you," Maria said. Her face was thoughtful. She was worrying about the old man. It was a cool evening, and he'd need his jacket. He didn't seem exactly destitute, but all the same, she couldn't help worrying. What if he didn't have enough money to buy another jacket? Would he be all right until Winston could get hold of him?

Maybe it was silly to worry about him so much, but the old man and his granddaughter had captured Maria's sympathy. She just hoped he would call Winston. She knew she'd keep feeling uneasy until he had his jacket back again.

"Now, what time does this wonderful lottery drawing take place?" Lila demanded, her long legs tucked under her as she sat on the Egberts'

27

living room sofa. Winston had dimmed the lights so the room would seem to be dramatically lit. Bowls of chips, pretzels, and cheese curls were set out, and everyone was getting into the spirit of the evening.

"Ten o'clock," Winston said, rubbing his hands together. "Now I want all of you to be as calm as you possibly can. I'm going to go into the kitchen for a minute. And when I come back, you know what I'll have in my very own hands?"

"We shudder to think," Bruce Patman said dryly.

"A pint of almond-mocha ice cream?" Enid asked hopefully, and everyone giggled.

"Nope! Guess again," Winston instructed.

"Something tells me it's going to be a small green lottery ticket," Jessica said.

"You're absolutely right. It's in the kitchen drawer, where I've been keeping it safe. Close your eyes and try not to get too excited. I'll be right back!" Winston exclaimed. He hurried into the kitchen, laughing.

But the next minute the smile faded from his face as he was rummaging in the kitchen drawer. Where was it? He'd left it right there on top of his mother's matchbooks. He began to dig furiously through the drawer, and then all of a sudden he remembered. "I took it out and put it in my pocket," he murmured. He hurried to the coat closet at the far end of the kitchen and yanked it open. His gaze fell on the navy blue

28

jacket, and an expression of horror crossed his face. The jacket! The old man had taken his jacket—and his lottery ticket was in the pocket.

Winston couldn't believe it. He'd gotten all his friends to come over, he'd gone to all that trouble, turning the whole thing into such a big production, and he'd lost the ticket! He felt like a prize idiot. What was he going to tell everyone? That he had managed to let some old man walk off with his jacket, and his lottery ticket just happened to be in the pocket? Crestfallen, he slipped his hand into the right-hand pocket of the old man's coat, where his ticket should have been. It was empty, of course. He felt incredibly disappointed.

"Winston?" Maria said, coming into the kitchen.

Winston was just about to explain what had happened when his fingers touched a bit of cardboard in the left-hand pocket of the navy jacket. His eyes widened as he grasped it in his fingers. It felt like the right size. He couldn't believe his eyes as he withdrew it. It was another ticket! Now what were the odds of *that*? Obviously fate had made some kind of connection between the old man and himself. He pulled the ticket out and turned to Maria without saying anything about it.

"It's almost time for the drawing!" Maria exclaimed. "We were wondering what was taking you so long."

"I've just been trying to calm my shattered nerves," Winston said jovially, slipping his arm around her and following her back into the living room, where Ollie Perold, the famous disc jockey, was just about to announce the winning number of that week's lottery.

"What's your ticket number, Winston?" Bruce asked, leaning forward to turn up the volume on the TV set. Ollie Perold was explaining that the jackpot for that week was up to twenty-five thousand dollars.

Winston glanced down at the old man's ticket. "Nine-six-five-eight-one-one," he said.

Frowning, Elizabeth glanced up at him. Had she heard him correctly? Weren't the first three numbers on the ticket 712? She never would have remembered if it weren't for that strange coincidence about Jeffrey's birthday. She made a mental note to ask Winston about it later.

"Ladies and gentlemen, it's the moment you've all been waiting for!" Ollie Perold announced triumphantly. He turned to face the viewing audience with a big smile. "Now as you all know, the jackpot has been growing. Today's winner will receive—yes, folks, it's true—twenty-five thousand dollars!"

This information was met with squeals and applause from everyone in the Egberts' living room. "Winston! Are they drawing the number?" Mrs. Egbert cried, hurrying into the living room. Mr. Egbert was right behind her, his expression both amused and curious. Everyone was literally on the edge of his seat. The tension mounted as Ollie leaned forward and took the envelope with that week's winning number inside from the technician. "OK, folks, hold on to your tickets!" he cried, ripping open the envelope. "The winning number is—are you listening? Are you checking your tickets? The winning number is nine-six-five-eight-one-one!"

Winston's mouth dropped open.

"Egbert! That's you!" Bruce yelled, jumping to his feet and snatching the ticket from Winston's hand. "God, he's really done it!" he cried to the rest of the room. "I can't believe it. The odds must've been about a million to one!"

Within seconds the entire room was in turmoil. Mr. and Mrs. Egbert looked stunned. Lila and Jessica were squealing and trying to get a look at the ticket. Maria was pale, her brown eyes wide, staring at Winston as if he were someone she had never seen before. Regina and Bruce hugged each other, then Winston, then each other again. Roger and Olivia were cheering loudly, and Nicholas kept slapping Winston on the back. Then Mr. Egbert flew into action racing to the phone to call the lottery number.

"I—I just can't believe it," Winston choked out, shocked. "I think—I don't know—you have to be eighteen to win. Dad, will you—"

But he never finished the sentence. Everyone was talking at once. Jessica wanted to know what he was going to do with the money. Lila was hugging Winston and acting as though she'd known he was going to win all along. Elizabeth and Jeffrey kept shaking their heads in disbelief, and Winston just stood absolutely still as if the whole thing were happening to someone else.

"I've got them on the phone!" Mr. Egbert exclaimed.

"Just a second—I've got to—ah, I've got to . . ." Winston's voice trailed off as he hurried out of the room. He needed to be alone, just to catch his breath. Just until he could sort out exactly what was going on.

He stared at his parents' familiar kitchen in total disbelief. That was it—965811. A winning ticket that suddenly represented twenty-five thousand dollars—more money than Winston had ever dreamed of in his entire life.

He couldn't believe it. He just couldn't believe it had happened. Suddenly he felt dizzy. He didn't know *what* he felt.

He had the winning ticket, all right. The only thing was, it wasn't his. Nobody knew that except Winston. And the question was, what on earth was he supposed to do now?

Four

"I can't believe it," Elizabeth said, taking the manila envelope out of the mailbox with trembling fingers. "It's come, Jessica—the material from the Interlochen School!"

The twins had just gotten home from school the next day, and as usual the very first thing Elizabeth had done was to rush for the mailbox. But that time her search wasn't in vain! She could barely believe it as she stared down at the large envelope, scrutinizing the foreign stamps. "Look how thick it is!" she exclaimed to Jessica. "They wouldn't send a letter saying I'm too late to apply in an envelope this size, would they?"

"Who knows?" Jessica said, looking gloomy. She hung over her sister's shoulder, examining the package. "Look at all those stamps," she said. "It looks like they sent it from Mars!"

"Come on," Elizabeth said eagerly. "Let's go inside and see what it says."

Ten minutes later the Wakefields' kitchen table was completely covered with brochures, applications, catalogs—all the material describing the Interlochen School. But the one piece of paper Elizabeth was concentrating on was the cover letter form Mr. Hummel, the headmaster.

"I can't believe how perfect this sounds," she murmured. "Jess, they actually have scholarships for the creative-writing program! Listen— 'The Margaret Sterne Memorial Prize for creative writing is presented in memory of Margaret Sterne, who was from California and studied at the Interlochen School in the nineteen-fifties. It is to be given to an eligible student for a full year of study in the English department. Included are three months of intensive writing workshops in the summer and nine months of combined creative writing and academic work in the senior year.' "

"I wonder who Margaret Sterne was," Jessica said darkly, pouring herself a glass of Diet Coke. "She was probably some poor girl who abandoned her family and came to a horrible end in the Alps somewhere."

Elizabeth frowned at her. "You happen to be wrong," she informed her sister. "Margaret Sterne was a talented young writer who died

34

prematurely of a terminal illness. It says right here that the Sterne family set up these scholarships in her name." Her eyes flicked over the tiny print describing the scholarship: "Applicants should have a demonstrated ability for creative writing. They must be female, between the ages of fifteen and seventeen and must be from California. They must show a commitment to scholarship and academic excellence, as well as embody the traits Margaret Sterne was known for: courage, persistence, dedication, and an involvement in community affairs."

"Gag," Jessica said, getting up to look in the cupboards. "No wonder this girl didn't make it to maturity. She sounds like she was more of a saint than a human being."

"Come on, Jess. I think the Sterne family has done a wonderful thing setting up this scholarship fund in her memory," Elizabeth defended. "Anyway, it's sure worth applying for!"

"That is, if you happen to embody courage, persistence, dedication, and be involved in community affairs," Jessica reminded her.

Elizabeth blushed. "So you think I shouldn't even try?" she asked.

Jessica sighed. "Of course you should!" she relented. "What worries me, Liz, is that you're absolutely perfect. I can't think of a better candidate. Which means they're going to interview you, find out that you're even saintlier than this Margaret Sterne was, and whisk you away to

Geneva." She looked really upset as she opened a package of Oreos. "And that'll be it, no more twin. The next time I see you, you'll have fallen in love with some shepherd or a yodeler or whatever, and you'll decide to live in Switzerland for the rest of your life."

Elizabeth ignored the prophecy. "Mr. Hummel says I have time to make the deadline for the creative-writing program," she said thoughtfully. "I'll need to have my records and transcripts sent to the Interlochen School as soon as possible, along with three letters of recommendation." She frowned. "I can ask Mr. Collins, of course." Mr. Collins, one of the most popular teachers at school, was the faculty advisor to *The Oracle* and taught English as well. She knew he would give her a strong recommendation. "But who else? Do you think I should ask Ms. Dalton? I like French, and that way they'll know I have some language skills."

"I'm sure half the faculty at school will be fighting to write you letters," Jessica said morosely, twisting the top off her Oreo and glaring down at it. "I can just imagine the letters now. They'll all go on and on about the work you've done demonstrating leadership—like the time you helped organize the carnival for the handicapped kids with Mrs. Morrow. Or the way you helped set up the foreign-language festival— And all the stuff you've done on *The Oracle*." She sighed. "It's hopeless. Absolutely hopeless."

36

Elizabeth scanned the letter again. "I also have to send three writing samples," she said thoughtfully. "I suppose I can send one of the pieces I've written for *The Oracle*. And maybe I can send that play I wrote about Elizabeth Barrett Browning—do you think that would be good enough?"

"Yes," Jessica said, popping the cookie in her mouth. "That's the whole problem, Lizzie. *Everything* you write is good enough."

"Mr. Collins might help me revise the short story I've been working on. That should do it for the writing part." Elizabeth opened the application package, her brow wrinkling as she glanced down at it. "What worries me is this thing about the home interview. Listen to this.

"In keeping with the highly personal nature of this scholarship, each candidate shall be interviewed both by a local representative—an alumnus from the Interlochen School—and by a member of the Sterne family to determine whether the applicant truly exhibits the characteristics required by the fellowship."

"So what?" Jessica said, reaching into the bag for another Oreo. "Tell me they're not just going to adore you, Liz. I mean, what are you afraid of? Your criminal record? Your terrible behavior in school?" She shook her head. "You're only totally perfect, that's all. No wonder you're worried about being interviewed."

"I'm supposed to call Patrick Sterne in San Diego," Elizabeth continued, taking out the small note appended to her application file. "He's the executor of the Sterne Fund. And he'll start the interviewing process right away." She looked up at Jessica, her eyes bright. "Jess, this is really happening! I can't believe it!"

"You're not the only one," Jessica said. "I just can't see why you're so happy about it. What's wrong, Liz? Are we all so horrible you can't stand the thought of living with us for another second?"

Elizabeth didn't answer. She was so wrapped up in the description of the writing program at the Interlochen School that she hadn't heard what her twin had said.

"Steve, we've got an emergency," Jessica said grimly. She was on the phone upstairs in her room, the door shut so no one could hear. Not that anyone in her family would ever walk into Jessica's room without what Mr. Wakefield called a "passport to chaos." Jessica liked her room, which she had painted chocolate brown, and which her family had nicknamed the "Hershey Bar." At the moment the better part of Jessica's wardrobe was strewn over her desk chair and the end of her bed, and it had taken her several minutes to find the phone. But that, as far as Jessica was concerned, was what a bedroom was for.

"What do you mean, 'emergency'?" Steven asked, alarmed. "This isn't like the last 'emergency,' is it, Jess?"

A few weeks earlier Jessica had called Steven home when she and Elizabeth had been convinced that Mrs. Wakefield was pregnant. The "emergency" had proven to be a false alarm, however, and now Steven was obviously on guard.

"No, Steven, this time it's really serious. It's Liz. She just got a pile of stuff from this man in Switzerland—Himmel or Hammel or whatever his name is. And it looks like there's a scholarship she was just *made* for. All expenses are paid for a year, and the applicants have to be ace writers and all-time perfect people. Just like Liz."

Steven cleared his throat. "Uh-oh. Have Mom and Dad found out yet?"

"They're downstairs talking to Liz about it right now," Jessica said. "They're going over all the application material together." She sounded stricken.

"Wow," Steven said. "You're right, Jess. It sounds like a first-class emergency."

"So what do we do?" Jessica wailed. "Steve, we can't let her go. There's no way I can make it around here without Liz. Besides," she added,

39

worried Steven would accuse her of being selfish, "who knows what could happen to her over there? The whole thing sounds creepy to me. We'd never get to see her, and she'd probably get completely ruined by all those snobs in boarding school." She twisted the phone cord up in anguish. "I bet she'll come home speaking German or something! Or smoking those gross little cigarettes like they do in old movies. And dragging us all to things like the *opera* or something."

"God forbid," Steven said, teasing her. "Jessica, you're the only person I know who makes culture sound like a fatal disease!"

"Boarding school is for kids with nowhere else to go," Jessica said, gathering steam. "Not for someone like Liz with a family who loves her. Steve, we've got to convince her not to apply. Because the minute she sends them her writing and her grades and everything, they'll give her every scholarship they've got!"

"You're right," Steven said thoughtfully. "But I don't think we should do anything drastic yet, Jess. Why don't we wait to hear what Mom and Dad have to say about the whole thing."

"OK," Jessica said. "But I think you should start thinking about it, Steve. You know Mom and Dad. They'll probably say something crazy like 'It might be a good experience' or something."

"Nah," Steven said, trying to assure her.

"They'll never let her go. Trust me, Jess. Remember what happened when I wanted to leave school to join Bob Rose's cruise ship? They'll probably tell her she can't even apply."

Jessica sighed. She hoped Steven was right, but she had a terrible feeling that he wasn't.

Elizabeth pushed her hair back with one hand. The expression in her blue-green eyes was distraught. "I don't understand why no one else seems excited about this," she complained to her parents. "This is the best opportunity in the whole world! Can't you imagine how wonderful it would be for me to get a chance to experience a new culture? To improve my French and start to learn German? Not to mention the opportunity to study with Nadia DeMann. She's one of the best writing teachers in the world, and she's actually part of the program at the Interlochen School."

Mrs. Wakefield looked upset. "We're just trying to understand *why* it's so important for you to go away next year, honey. It seems to me that college will come so quickly, anyway. Don't you want the chance to graduate with the rest of your class? And what about your friends here?"

"We're only trying to think of things that you might have overlooked," Mr. Wakefield assured her, patting her hand. "It isn't that we're not excited for you, honey. The program sounds good, and I can't think of anyone better suited for this Margaret Sterne prize than you."

Elizabeth took a deep breath. "But you still think it's crazy," she said unhappily. "You still think I'm wrong even to apply."

The Wakefields exchanged uneasy glances. "We didn't say that, Liz," Mrs. Wakefield reminded her. "I think what we're saying is that we just want the chance to think about it a little bit more before we decide anything. Remember how concerned we were when Steven wanted to leave school to join his roommate on that cruise ship? We just want to be sure you aren't being impulsive, as he was."

"That's right," Mr. Wakefield agreed. "We have a lot more talking and thinking to do before we can reach a decision as big as this one."

"Maybe we could call the Interlochen School tomorrow, and you could talk to Mr. Hummel," Elizabeth suggested. "Do you think that might help settle things?" She couldn't bear to think that her parents were imagining her plans were as impetuous or half-baked as her brother's had been.

"That's not such a bad idea," Mr. Wakefield said thoughtfully. "I can try to reach him tomorrow morning from the office. I should be able to get him at his home around dinnertime." Meanwhile, I think we all need to sleep on this. Remember, Liz, this is kind of a shock to us.

We hadn't thought we'd be losing one of our little girls so soon."

"Oh, Dad," Elizabeth said impatiently. "You wouldn't be losing me! And I'm not little, either," she added.

Her parents smiled at each other as Elizabeth got up from the table where they had been talking. She had the distinct impression they thought she *was* little. She couldn't help wishing they were a bit more enthusiastic about the program.

After all, the Margaret Sterne Memorial Prize had essentially turned a fantasy into a reality. She knew it would be very competitive, but it seemed as though she had a chance. A real chance.

Why wasn't anyone else excited for her? Even Enid had been decidedly lukewarm when Elizabeth had called her before dinner. Elizabeth had told her all about the program, outlining the courses she would take, the prizes Nadia DeMann had won for her novels, and describing the breathtaking pictures of the chaletlike dormitories where she would live. "Enid, it's like something out of a fairy tale!" she had concluded, breathless with excitement.

"It sounds terrific," Enid had said flatly. "Liz, did you understand the assignment we got today in chemistry? I had to leave early to go to the office, and Caroline Pearce couldn't really explain it to me."

43

Elizabeth had understood then that the discussion about Switzerland was closed. And she couldn't help feeling a little bit hurt. Enid was supposed to be her best friend. Didn't that mean she ought to be as excited about the Interlochen School as Elizabeth was?

Well, she thought as she started to climb the stairs, Enid wasn't the only one who seemed less than one hundred percent enthusiastic about her plans. Jessica was being impossible about the whole thing. And she could hardly say her parents had been exactly overjoyed.

Thank heavens for Jeffrey, she thought, hurrying up the last stairs so she could call him and tell him the news. At least Jeffrey was behind her.

Five

"Winston! Winston!" Lila Fowler came hurrying up to Winston in the hall, her face animated. "I can't believe what a celebrity you've turned into," she cooed, slipping her arm through his. "Isn't it fun—reporters coming to school to interview you and everything?" She lowered her lashes suggestively. "I'm sure if they want to talk to any of your *really* close friends about you that I could always tell them a thing or two."

Winston disentangled himself. He felt like asking Lila when they had become such good friends. But there was no point. Everyone was acting so different to him since the news had broken about his lottery ticket. Even his parents seemed to have flipped.

He could barely believe it was only Thursday—

just two days since he had picked up the wrong jacket in Drake's. Everything since then had been topsy-turvy. The minute he realized what had happened with the ticket, he felt as if he had stepped into somebody else's life—as if he had taken on a terrible weight. What was he going to do? It was all he could think about. And the worst thing was that nobody else knew what was happening inside him. His parents were overjoyed. When Mr. Egbert had called the lottery office, a woman named Robin Royce had congratulated them at length. Apparently, although minors couldn't buy tickets themselves, they could certainly win. Winston was the official winner! She said she would let the publicity people know at once; they in turn would notify the newspapers and television stations.

The news was out: Winston Egbert had won the lottery!

The next step, according to Ms. Royce, was for the Egberts to come to the main lottery office downtown and fill out a form. That form, along with the winning ticket, would be processed; a certain amount of money would be withheld for taxes and social security, and the rest of the money would be set up in trust for Winston, his parents acting as financial guardians. Mr. Egbert went right out to buy a bottle of champagne.

Winston knew he had to tell his parents the truth, but they were so excited on Tuesday night that he just couldn't. And the longer he waited, the harder it became.

By Wednesday the news had spread through school like wildfire. Every single person Winston saw in school slapped him on the back or shook his hand, demanding to know what it felt like to be a big winner. Everyone started teasing him about loans. By the end of the day people had even started to call him nicknames like "Big Win." His teachers treated him differently—even Maria seemed to be acting like a stranger. The whole thing was getting to him. It would be one thing if he could sit back and really enjoy his new status. But he just felt terrible. Sooner or later the old man would come forward, and then what?

Deep inside it wasn't even the fear of being discovered that was troubling him. Winston knew the money wasn't really his. But how could he bask in all this glory, tell the reporters about his plans to use the money for college, or make jokes about getting rich quick with friends at school knowing that poor old man had *really* won?

Winston glanced uneasily at his watch. He still had twenty minutes left of his study hall, and he knew it would be a good idea to look over chapter five in his history book before the quiz Mr. Fellows was giving the next hour. He ducked into the library, looked around for a spare seat, and found a free carrel open right next to Elizabeth Wakefield.

"Liz!" he said, pleased to see her. He kept his voice down so he wouldn't disturb anyone else. "How's the application coming?"

Elizabeth smiled. "I'm so wrapped up in it I can't think about anything else," she confessed. "Did you hear about this Margaret Sterne Memorial Prize I'm applying for?"

Winston laughed. "Are you kidding? You're the most famous person in school the past two days—after me. All anyone's talking about anymore is how you're about to get a scholarship to spend a year in Switzerland—and how I'm about to join in the life of the bright young jet-set crowd."

Elizabeth looked serious. "I don't even know if I really have a chance," she said. "I just reached Patrick Sterne this morning—he's the executor of the family trust, and he's the one who's got to check me out. You know, make sure I'm really a decent person. So there's a chance that things could go wrong."

Winston fiddled with his notebook. "I'm sure you'll do fine," he said loyally. "You're the most decent person *I've* ever met." He felt a sudden wave of gloom. What would Patrick Sterne have to say about a shady character like himself—virtually stealing a winning lottery ticket out of the hand of a poor old man?

He felt sick to his stomach. This was it, he

48

decided. Right after school he was going over to Drake's to see if the old man had checked back about his jacket. If he had, Winston was going to go right over to his house and tell him the truth about his ticket.

"You know, Winston," Elizabeth said suddenly. "I meant to ask you something the other night. I know this sounds strange, but I happened to notice the first few numbers on your ticket—because they were the same as Jeffrey's birthday, written out as numbers—seven-twelve. But the number on the ticket that won on Tuesday started with nine-sixty-five. Did you have two tickets, or am I losing my mind?"

Winston felt as if he had been caught in a trap. "My dad gave me two," he said, without stopping to think. "I just showed you guys one because I didn't want you to think I was trying to increase my chances."

"Oh," Elizabeth said, smiling. "I thought that must be what happened." She turned back to her application essay without further comment.

She believes me, Winston thought miserably. *She has no idea what a rotten liar I am.* He was more determined than ever to come clean that very afternoon. It still wasn't too late to give back the twenty-five thousand dollars to its rightful owner.

It took Winston almost twenty minutes to find the house on Fenno Street, a narrow avenue in the poorest part of the Sweet Valley. He had gotten the old man's name and address from the man behind the cash register at Drake's: Jack Oliver, 15 Fenno Street. Apparently the old man had come in Wednesday morning and left Winston's jacket. Sure enough, the lottery ticket—his own lottery ticket—was still in the pocket. The first part of his task was completed—now he just had to find Mr. Oliver and explain what had happened.

The house on Fenno Street was smaller than Winston expected, and its exterior was in serious need of repainting and repair. But there was something charming about the house as well. Geraniums were growing in pots outside the windows, and it was apparent that every effort had been made to make the house homey. Winston shifted his weight from one foot to the other as he rang the doorbell. He just hoped Jack Oliver wasn't going to bite his head off for trying to make off with his ticket!

A minute later the door opened. Mr. Oliver was wearing a faded flannel shirt and a pair of trousers that looked too big for him. "Hello," he said softly. "Are you here to sell something? Because I'm afraid—"

"Mr. Oliver? My name is Winston Egbert. I left my name with the man at Drake's the other night. I'm the one who took your jacket by mistake," Winston explained quickly.

"Oh! Come in, come in," Mr. Oliver said,

opening the door wider. "I'm so sorry," he added, taking a pair of glasses out of his pocket and putting them on to get a better look at Winston. "I just assume everyone who comes by these days is a salesman. Not very polite of me, is it?"

"Uh—no. I mean, yes. It's OK," Winston said, feeling as if he had no idea what to say.

"Please come in and have a glass of apple cider," the old man urged him. "To tell you the truth, I wouldn't mind a minute or two of company. And I want to thank you for going out of your way to bring me back my jacket." He took the coat from Winston with an appreciative smile. "Truth was, I was more than a little sorry to have misplaced it. I find I get so much colder than I used to! Old age does something rotten to your circulation, you know that?"

Winston swallowed. He couldn't help looking around him as he followed Mr. Oliver down the narrow hallway to the living room. The furnishings were pretty basic: an old sofa, a few little tables, a TV set that looked as if it might have been one of the first ones ever invented. Everything was clean and neat, but the furniture was positively threadbare.

Mr. Oliver came out of the kitchen in a minute, carrying a tray with a pitcher on it and two glasses. "Looking at my little granddaughter?" he asked, pointing to a photograph on the wall of the little girl Winston and Maria had seen

51

with Mr. Oliver in Drake's. "Sweetest little creature in the world," he added, pouring Winston some cider. "I'd like to give her the world." He shook his head. "Sometimes it breaks your heart, having a little girl like that who asks you for things. I never once regretted not being a rich man until Lisa came along. Now I wish . . ." His voice trailed off sadly.

Winston bit his lip, feeling terrible. His eye caught some lottery tickets on the table nearest the TV. "You play the lottery?" he asked casually.

Mr. Oliver nodded. "I guess you could call me a 'season subscriber.' I get one every week. But to tell you the truth, I've kind of gone off the whole idea. Doesn't seem that much fun anymore. I haven't even been following the numbers for the past few weeks." He sighed. "I think I'm just going to let the whole thing go. That way"—his face brightened—"that way, I might be able to help Lisa's mom—that's my daughter, Karen—save up some money so Lisa can go to riding camp this summer. The little thing just loves horses. She wants to go to camp more than anything in the world, but Karen can't afford it. I figure if I stop wasting money on those lottery tickets, I might be able to help her out."

Winston gulped. Mr. Oliver didn't even know he'd won the lottery! Didn't that change everything? It wasn't as if he felt cheated or anything.

And it *was* twenty-five thousand dollars. Winston suddenly felt uncertain about everything. Before he had come over to meet Mr. Oliver, everything seemed perfectly clear. But now, he thought, it would be crazy to give the old man his money.

Jack Oliver would never know if Winston kept it. All he had to do was keep quiet, and the lottery jackpot was his.

"Listen, everyone," Elizabeth said, wandering into the living room that night with a book in her hand. Her parents and Jessica looked up from watching television as Elizabeth faced them.

"I know this is going to sound kind of strange," Elizabeth said, "but I've been thinking more about what it's going to be like when Mr. Sterne comes over here to meet all of you. He hasn't given me a day yet, but it'll be soon—probably next week. He's going to ask you all sorts of things about me, and I just thought"—she cleared her throat—"you know, maybe we could kind of rehearse."

"Rehearse?" Jessica repeated. "In the middle of my favorite program? Liz, are you out of your mind?"

"I'm sure we'll do just fine improvising, dear," Mrs. Wakefield said gently. "We'll try not to act like ogres."

"Listen, I don't want to sound like I'm giving you *advice* or anything," Elizabeth continued, "but I was talking to Mr. Collins today, and he seemed to think that Mr. Sterne will want to hear about how well rounded I am. Things like musical interests and keeping up with current events and—"

"How about things like letting your family watch TV in peace?" Jessica snapped.

Elizabeth sighed. "Fine, I can take a hint," she said, wandering out of the living room and picking up the phone in the kitchen. She wished her family would show a little more concern about Mr. Sterne's interview. After all, her whole future was on the line.

"Jeffrey? It's me," she said a minute later when Jeffrey had picked up the phone. She tried all day to find a couple of minutes alone with him, but he had been so busy the last few days and she had been so wrapped up in her application, that they missed each other at lunch, during study hall, and after school.

"Hi!" Jeffrey said warmly. "How are you? I feel like you and I are fated to miss each other at every turn." His voice sounded husky. "I wish I could see you tonight. I have something I want to give you."

Elizabeth sank down into a chair. "Really? What is it?" she asked.

"It's going to have to wait until tomorrow night. I'm taking you somewhere special," he told her. "I know you're going to love it."

Elizabeth bit her lip. "Tomorrow night? Jeffrey, I was going to work on my short story this weekend. I've got to get it revised and in shape to send it off first thing Monday morning." She twisted up the phone cord, feeling anxious. "Can we postpone the 'somewhere special'? I was hoping you could help me with my story."

Jeffrey was silent for a moment. "Well, if that's what you really want to do," he said at last, disappointed. "Are you sure there's no way we could work on the story on Saturday instead?"

"I promised Mr. Collins I'd baby-sit for Teddy on Saturday," Elizabeth said. Teddy was Mr. Collins's six-year-old son. After Mr. Collins and his wife divorced, he had been granted custody of their child, and Elizabeth frequently sat for Teddy on the weekends.

"OK," Jeffrey said. "We'll postpone the 'somewhere special' then."

"Jeffrey," Eizabeth said, as if it had just occurred to her, "I wonder if Mr. Sterne will want to talk to you when he comes to school next week. You think he'll want to ask you questions about me?"

"Who knows? I'd be happy to tell him anything he wants to know." Jeffrey laughed. "I can personally attest to all sorts of qualities. 'Elizabeth Wakefield is the softest, the sexiest, the most romantic girl I've ever been in love with,' " he said.

"Jeffrey! You can't say things like that," Elizabeth exclaimed.

"Trust me," Jeffrey said dryly. "If anyone asks about you, Liz, I'll just hand them a résumé listing all the prizes you've ever won."

"That won't do, either," Elizabeth said.

"I'm just kidding," Jeffrey objected. "Liz, are you losing your sense of humor over this whole thing?"

Elizabeth didn't answer. She didn't think she was. She thought the problem was that no one else was taking her application seriously enough.

Clearly she was going to have to redouble her efforts over the next few days, or there might well be some misunderstandings when Mr. Sterne came to Sweet Valley to find out about her!

Six

"I thought you were going to stay home tonight and get Jeffrey to help you with your short story," Enid said loudly, trying to be heard over the music in the Beach Disco. A bunch of students from Sweet Valley High had organized a spur-of-the-moment TGIF party at the popular dancing spot overlooking the ocean. And in the end Elizabeth had let Jeffrey convince her to go along with him for an hour or two.

"We're going to leave early," Elizabeth said, glancing down at her watch. It was already ten-thirty. She didn't want to be a pain, but she knew she should get home fairly soon or she'd never be able to get up early enough the next day to have a productive morning. Elizabeth really wanted her application to be perfect.

"Let's go outside so we can talk," Enid said suddenly. "It's so noisy in here!" The Droids, Sweet Valley High's own rock band, were playing one of their latest hits—a song called "Something Sure" with a pounding bass line.

"Good idea," Elizabeth said. Jeffrey was deep in conversation with Winston, Regina, and Bruce in the corner, so she thought it would be a good time to catch up with her best friend.

"I've barely seen you the last few days," Enid said as they strolled together down the wooden steps leading to the beach. It was cool outside, but the breeze from the ocean felt wonderful after the hot, crowded disco.

"I know. I've been so busy with this application," Elizabeth explained. "Enid, I've been meaning to talk to you about this, anyway. I have a feeling that Patrick Sterne—the man who's coming to school to talk to Mr. Collins and my other teachers—is going to want to talk to a few of my best friends as well. You know, just asking things like how long we've known each other and what sort of impressions of me you have." Elizabeth peered at Enid. "You know what I mean?"

Enid giggled. "It sounds to me like you don't want me to bring up your drug habit. Or your wild behavior with older men. Or— "

Elizabeth looked stricken. "Come on, Enid. That isn't funny! This man is going to want a character reference. He may ask you some strange questions."

"Like what?"

"Oh, I don't know. Like if I have a bad temper or if you've ever seen me handle a situation in a way that you found less than commendable. Things like that."

Enid patted Elizabeth reassuringly on the arm. "Listen, Liz, I don't know what this guy is going to be like, but I'm sure he really wants to get to know you—and he won't be trying to snoop around digging up peculiar information from your friends. But if he asks me about anything like that, I'll just tell him the truth." She gave Elizabeth a quick hug. "You're the world's most generous, loving friend. And I've always admired everything you do and say."

Elizabeth frowned. "You don't want to go overboard, though," she said anxiously. "I mean, you don't want to give him the impression that I'm not human, or that you're trying to cover something up by exaggerating my strengths."

"Liz," Enid said, looking annoyed, "you don't have to coach me. I think the world of you, and that's obviously going to come through if anyone asks me anything about you." She frowned. "I think you should relax about the whole thing. To tell you the truth, I think we're all going to do just fine in front of this Mr. Sterne. Trust us!"

Elizabeth sighed. "I know I'm being silly, Enid.

But I think Mr. Sterne's interviews are going to have a huge impact on the final decision. And I just want to make sure everything goes smoothly."

Enid dragged the tip of her shoe in the sand. "You sure seem excited about this whole thing," she said flatly. "All I ever hear from you is talk about Switzerland." Her jaw muscles tightened slightly. "I guess Sweet Valley seems kind of dull to you these days, huh?"

"Of course it doesn't!" Elizabeth exclaimed. "It's just that the Interlochen School really seems like a dream come true. It would give me a chance to learn all about a culture that's foreign to me—a chance to study with first-rate writers—and more than anything else, to soak up all that inspiration." Her eyes shone. "I think if I manage to win a scholarship and actually go, this could be the turning point in my whole life."

Enid shook her head. "I think you're going off the deep end, Liz. I know I probably shouldn't say anything," she added quickly, "but you and I are best friends, and we've helped each other through some rough times. We've always been honest with each other, right?"

"Right," Elizabeth said tensely. "But I can't see what you mean about going off the deep end. I happen to think that everyone I know is being a little unfair. Not one person has supported me about this application—not my parents, not Jessica, not even you!"

"Maybe that's because we don't want you to go away," Enid cried. "Did you ever think of that?"

"That's pretty selfish," Elizabeth said angrily. "It seems to me that part of being a best friend is wanting what's best for the other person."

"I'm not even convinced that Switzerland is the best place for you," Enid objected. "I can see how exotic it all sounds, but would it really *inspire* you? Mr. Collins is always going on about how important it is to be inspired by common, everyday experiences. Why do you need to stare at the Alps to write?"

Elizabeth's face flushed with anger. "You're not even trying to understand," she said, accusing her friend. "Forget it, Enid. It's obvious that none of you really cares about what's best for me." Her eyes flashed. "But I'm still going ahead with it. I just hope Mr. Sterne thinks I deserve the scholarship so I can show you all how wrong you are!"

She spun on her heel, leaving Enid staring unhappily after her, as she hurried back inside to find Jeffrey.

Elizabeth had had enough. She wanted to go back home and work on her story. Right then she felt betrayed, by her family and by Enid as well. And she was going to try twice as hard to make sure the Interlochen School realized how special a candidate she really was.

*   *   *

61

Enid felt terrible all day Saturday about her argument with Elizabeth. It wasn't like them to quarrel. In fact, she couldn't remember the last disagreement they'd had. She tried reaching Elizabeth, but Mrs. Wakefield said she was at the public library and was going to go over to sit for Teddy Collins from there. It looked as if their truce was going to have to wait.

This made Enid all the more pleased to bump into Jeffrey downtown. Jeffrey didn't look overwhelmingly happy himself. He was frowning at a shop display when Enid caught sight of him holding a small package in his hands. When Enid came up to say hello, he looked about a million miles away.

"Are you OK, Jeffrey?" Enid asked. "You seem kind of distracted."

"Oh—I was just looking at that backdrop," Jeffrey explained, somewhat sheepishly. The store window featured a pair of mannequins in front of a poster-board landscape of the Alps. "It's funny how popular Switzerland seems to be. No wonder Liz is so obsessed with it."

"Jeffrey, can we talk?" Enid asked him seriously. "I'm really worried about her. We got into a big argument last night—did she tell you?"

Jeffrey nodded. "Yeah, but I think that's pretty standard lately. I ended up arguing with her, too. She was pretty upset by the time I dropped her off."

Enid shook her head. "I'm really upset, too. I

want to be supportive and everything, but I think she's gone way overboard on this Switzerland thing." Her green eyes were intent on Jeffrey's. "Don't you think there's got to be some way to get her to change her mind?"

Jeffrey frowned. "No, not really. That was the way I felt earlier this week, but now it seems to me that this is what she really wants. And I think we owe it to her to back her one hundred percent."

Enid was thoughtful for a minute. "Maybe you're right," she said softly. "I guess I haven't been a very good friend. I've just been thinking about myself and how lonely I'll be without her—not about what Elizabeth wants." She sighed. "I feel really bad now."

"Do you want to see what I bought Liz this morning as a good-luck present?" Jeffrey took a small jewelry box out of the paper bag and opened it, showing Enid the tiny pearl pin that Elizabeth had admired earlier that week. "I'm going to take it over to her tonight while she's sitting for Teddy. I'm hoping it'll be a peace token—so she'll know I'm really behind her."

Enid's eyes shone. "Oh, Jeffrey—it's gorgeous! She's going to love it," she exclaimed. She looked hard at him, a thought occurring to her. "You know, I'd like to give Elizabeth a peace offering, too. Do you think she'd like it if I made her a scrapbook filled with pictures and souvenirs from the things we've done together? It could be a memory book for when she goes away."

"That's a fantastic idea," Jeffrey said. "I'm sure she'd love it. Maybe I can help you put it together. I've got tons of pictures from parties and things—ones I've taken myself." Jeffrey was an excellent photographer and had joined the photo staff of *The Oracle* to publish some of his work.

"Let's get started right away. Can you work on it this afternoon?"

"I don't see why not," Jeffrey said.

Enid could tell the idea appealed to him a great deal. And she knew it was partly because *action*—of any sort—seemed to dispel the frustrating sense that there was nothing they could do to stop Elizabeth from leaving them for good.

Winston took a deep breath. The people in the lottery office had him on hold, and he was listening to some kind of terrible recorded music, waiting for Robin Royce to come to the phone.

"Hello? This is Ms. Royce, the department manager," she said. "Can I help you?"

Winston gulped. "I'm doing a project on the lottery for school," he said rapidly. "My name is Jason Armstrong. I was wondering what would happen if someone won the lottery with a ticket that wasn't really his."

Ms. Royce wasn't being as friendly as she'd been to Winston when he spoke to her about the winning ticket. "What do you mean, 'not really his'?" she asked in a crisp voice.

"Well, say someone finds a ticket. Or gets one by accident. Or—"

"We don't ask for proof of ownership," she told him. "How could we? We can verify where a ticket was sold, but we can't keep track of who bought it. As far as we're concerned, the person who holds the winning ticket is the winner."

"Thanks," Winston said. He said goodbye and hung up.

Some help, he thought miserably. All she had told him was that the ticket he'd found in Mr. Oliver's jacket was his for the taking. It was his twenty-five thousand dollars, and that was all there was to it.

So why did he feel so terrible about the whole thing?

Seven

Jessica was up in her bedroom on Sunday with the door closed, taking advantage of the fact that Elizabeth was downstairs to sneak a quick phone call to Steven. "It's me," she announced when his roommate had called him from the student lounge.

"Me, who?" Steven asked.

"Jessica!" she snapped. "Who did you think? Steve, listen—we've got a real problem on our hands."

"No, we don't," Steven informed her. "I told you I was going to come up with a plan, didn't I?"

"Yeah, but things are really deteriorating," Jessica complained. "Mom and Dad seem to have caved in completely. As far as I can tell, they think it's all systems go for Liz to take off to Interlochen. They keep saying that she's old enough to know what's best for herself. It's really awful."

"It figures Mom and Dad would say something like that," Steven said. "Especially when it comes to Liz. She's always been so sensible that they probably feel reluctant to stand in her way."

"So why aren't you panicking?" Jessica wailed. "Steve, I can't bear the thought of her taking off this summer and staying away for an entire year! Can you imagine how rotten my senior year would be without Liz?"

"Calm down," Steven said. "I told you—I came up with a plan. If you'd stop wailing for just a second, I could even tell it to you."

"OK," Jessica said, mollified. "What is it?"

"Look, this guy Sterne is coming to the house to check Liz out, right?"

"He's coming to the house on Thursday and to school on Friday," Jessica confirmed. "He called this afternoon."

"Hmm," Steven said, thinking. "OK, now here's what we do then. I'll come home Wednesday night. I don't have any classes Thursday, and Friday's tutorials can be skipped for something this important. That way you and I will be around Thursday to make sure Mr. Sterne gets the *right impression* of Elizabeth's family."

"What do you mean?" Jessica demanded.

"I mean," Steven said, "that you and I are going to have to make Mr. Sterne realize that Liz isn't the right girl for the Margaret Sterne Memorial Prize. All it'll take is one obnoxious twin sister and a depraved older brother to make him run in the other direction."

Jessica's eyes began to twinkle. "So you mean we'll sabotage her interview by acting like total jerks?"

"Exactly. Not just like jerks, but like people with so little moral fiber that Sterne will decide there's no way Liz can be as wholesome as she seems."

"You're a genius!" Jessica shrieked. She dropped her voice, remembering Elizabeth and her parents downstairs. "You know what?" she added, inspired. "I don't see why we couldn't carry the same thing on at school—on an even wider scale. Why not draft people to help us give Liz all the bad press we can. I know Lila will help. And if you put pressure on her, maybe Cara will, too." Cara Walker was one of Jessica's best friends and had been dating Steven for quite some time.

"That's a great idea," Steven said warmly. "You see, Jess, I told you we'd think of something!"

Jessica's brow was furrowed as she tried to rack her brains for ways to show Patrick Sterne how rotten her twin was.

She had to admit she liked her brother's plan. She just hoped that it would work!

Elizabeth frowned as she looked around the crowded lunchroom. She was supposed to have met Jeffrey there almost ten minutes before, but she couldn't see him anywhere. And it wasn't like him to be late.

Her hand flew automatically up to the pearl pin she was wearing on the lapel of her blazer. She still couldn't believe Jeffrey had bought it for her. At least a dozen people had stopped to compliment her on it. *I'll be sure to take it with me if I go to Switzerland*, she thought dreamily. Elizabeth had no intention of forgetting Jeffrey while she was away. In fact, she had a feeling that distance would work in their favor—they had such a strong relationship and they supported each other so wholeheartedly. She would wear the pin wherever she want and know that Jeffrey's love was still real and alive, however far apart they were.

Her reverie was shattered by the unwelcome sound of Lila Fowler's voice. "Liz! What a pretty little pin," Lila said, peering at it with eyes as sharp as an appraiser's. "Why don't you come keep me company? I hate eating lunch by myself, and Jessica's taking forever to join me here."

"Oh, I'm waiting for Jeffrey," Elizabeth told her, glad to have an excuse.

Lila raised her eyebrows. "You are? That's funny. I just saw him in the parking lot with Enid. They were getting into his car, as a matter of fact."

Elizabeth wrinkled her brow. Enid? Getting into Jeffrey's car? She wondered where they could be going in the middle of the day. And it wasn't like Jeffrey not to show up when they had agreed to have lunch together. She knew her confusion was apparent.

"Don't let it bug you," Lila advised, tucking her arm conspiratorially through Elizabeth's and steering her over to a free table. "I'm sure it's all *much* more innocent than it looked."

Elizabeth had to laugh. Lila saw intrigue anyplace. As if anything could possibly be going on between Enid and Jeffrey. "I trust them," she said lightly, sliding into an empty chair. "I'm just sorry to have missed Jeffrey, that's all."

"So," Lila said her eyes bright, "you mean you don't ever worry that Enid might still be interested in Jeffrey? Ater all she was mad about him when he first moved here."

Elizabeth reddened slightly. It was true that Enid had fallen for Jeffrey when he first arrived at Sweet Valley High. In fact, Lila had, too. Elizabeth had gotten to know Jeffrey when she went to bat for Enid, trying to convince him to get to know her friend better. Jeffrey had joined the staff of *The Oracle* as a photographer, and as he and Elizabeth had spent increasing amounts

70

of time together it became apparent that his affections lay not with Enid or Lila, but with Elizabeth herself.

"Enid doesn't feel anything for Jeffrey anymore," Elizabeth said calmly, watching Lila take her lunch out of a bag. Only Lila Fowler would bring take-out sushi for lunch, she thought smiling to herself.

"I'm surprised to hear you say that," Lila said, arranging her sushi before her with care. "It seems to me that after Enid was *so* nuts about him . . . And then it *does* seem like they've been inseparable lately. But I'm probably making something out of nothing," she added thoughtfully, popping a cucumber role into her mouth.

Elizabeth frowned. "What do you mean, inseparable?" she demanded. "I didn't think they'd been spending that much time together."

"Of course you didn't," Lila agreed. "They're being kind of secretive about the whole thing. In fact I ran into the two of them in the lounge just before school this morning. They had their heads bent over something—I couldn't see what it was—and they jumped about a mile when I came into the room." Lila sighed, shaking her head. "Of course if *I* were you, I'd be insanely jealous. But that's the thing about you, Liz. You're so—I don't know, so *trusting*."

Elizabeth suddenly lost her appetite. Jeffrey

71

and Enid? It wasn't possible. There had to be some kind of logical explanation.

But then what were the two of them doing taking off together in the middle of the day in Jeffrey's car? And why hadn't Jeffrey said anything to her about canceling their lunch date?

Elizabeth didn't know *what* to think. But she felt distinctly uneasy for the rest of the lunch hour.

Jeffrey felt bad about missing lunch with Elizabeth. In fact, nothing but the scrapbook he and Enid were making for Elizabeth could possibly have convinced him to miss the date. He and Enid had been hard at work putting photographs into the leather-bound scrapbook they'd bought Elizabeth during their study hall that morning when Enid became convinced that the glue they were using smelled funny and wouldn't work. After some good-hearted debate, they agreed to run out to a store during lunch and pick up a different kind.

"Dear Liz," Jeffrey scribbled on a sheet of loose-leaf paper. "I've got to run an errand with Enid, so I'm going to have to miss lunch. I love you—promise to explain later! Yours, Jeffrey."

He tucked the note into one of the slats on her locker. He was sure she'd understand—and, anyway, the errand wouldn't take long. He made sure the note was tucked in far enough so it wouldn't fall out, then hurried down the hall to meet Enid.

"I hope Liz found my note," Jeffrey said to Enid as he pulled his car into the parking lot in front of the stationery store. "I don't want her thinking I stood her up."

"I'm sure she found it. Didn't you put it in her locker?" Enid asked.

Jeffrey nodded. "I hope she likes the scrapbook," he added. "When do you think we should give it to her?"

Enid got out of the car. "Well, at the rate it's going, it'll take us awhile to finish it," she said. "Jeffrey, thanks so much for coming with me. That glue we were using just wasn't right—it'll be much better if we get a different kind."

"Yeah, and doing it now means we can work on the scrapbook during a free period today." Jeffrey followed Enid into the store, a smile playing about his lips.

He couldn't wait to surprise Elizabeth with the scrapbook. He knew she was going to love it!

What he didn't know was that a group of sophomore boys had snatched the note out of Elizabeth's locker and thrown it out.

Winston walked to the back of an aisle in Fine's, the brand-new toy store downtown. He couldn't believe how many dolls there were.

They all looked alike to him, too. How was he supposed to guess what kind of doll a little girl like Lisa would like?

His eyes fell on a beautiful ballerina doll, almost a foot tall, with long, flaxen hair. The doll came with a trunk filled with clothes. When Winston saw the price tag he couldn't believe it. How could a doll cost so much?

But he had the money, he reminded himself. The check had been issued by the state lottery and put into trust for him until he turned eighteen. In the meantime his parents had agreed that he could use the interest money to supplement his allowance. *Supplement* was the wrong word—the interest money was five times what his allowance had been! It came to almost fifty dollars a week. The doll would cost a whole week's interest, but Winston wanted—no, *needed* to buy it. He wanted to leave it for Lisa.

"I'd like to have this delivered, please," he told the store manager. "But I want it to be a surprise. Can that be arranged? I'd like to attach a card to it but no name."

"Sure," the manager said, smiling. "No problem. Just write whatever you want on this card. We'll have to charge you for delivering it, but we'll be happy to do it."

"Oh, don't worry about the money," Winston said, picking up the pen he'd been handed and trying to decide what to write. "For Lisa,

74

From a friend who hopes she likes ballerinas,"
he wrote.

He hoped Mr. Oliver would be happy when
the doll arrived for his grandchild. But at the
same time, he knew it wasn't fair. If Mr. Oliver
had his winning ticket, Lisa could go to the
riding camp she wanted. A doll—even a beautiful, expensive doll like that one—couldn't make
up for a whole summer!

Winston sighed as he walked away from the
cash register. He racked his brains for ways to
assuage his guilt. The idea of buying the doll
had come to him right in the middle of history
class that day. He'd been thrilled because it
seemed like the perfect thing to do.

But now it felt like an empty gesture. It felt as
if he were trying to make up for a huge, glaring
omission with something tiny and insignificant.

Winston couldn't ever remember feeling so
torn. He had a choice to make. Either he kept
the lottery money and continued feeling rotten,
or he came forward and admitted what had
happened—giving Mr. Oliver back his twenty-
five thousand dollars—and became the laugh-
ingstock of the entire town!

Eight

Elizabeth frowned at herself in her mirror. She had taken extra care to look nice that morning, and she thought the effort had paid off. She was wearing a new velvet ribbon on her blond ponytail, a plaid jumper, and a Victorian lace blouse that looked old-fashioned and pretty. She hoped Jeffrey noticed the pearl pin at her throat. She had worn it every day since Saturday.

The truth was, she hadn't seen that much of Jeffrey lately. Mostly it was her own fault. She had been so busy working on her application, and the time they *had* spent together they went over her writing samples. But Elizabeth had been especially preoccupied since her talk with Lila Fowler the day before at lunchtime. Not that she thought Lila had any business suggesting there was anything going on between Enid and Jeffrey. That was crazy! Enid was her dearest friend, and Jeffrey—well, Jeffrey just wouldn't play around on her. Besides, he insisted that he had left her a note. It must've gotten lost somehow. He hadn't stood her up on purpose!

She touched the pearl pin and started thinking. Of course, things were different now. She was talking about going away for a long, long time, and Jeffrey must be wondering what things would be like once they were separated. If she won the Margaret Sterne Memorial Prize, if she really left Sweet Valley, what would happen then? She couldn't imagine Jeffrey going out with someone else—least of all Enid. But she had to admit that it would be unreasonable to expect him to sit home and wait for her.

And she had to admit that she sometimes wondered what would happen if she met some glamorous European boy at Interlochen. Someone who could take her skiing in the Alps, who knew lots of languages. Maybe someone who wanted to be a writer, as she did.

In truth, Elizabeth *had* occasionally wondered. But she loved Jeffrey, and she certainly didn't want to lose him! She'd just have to make an effort to make him realize how special he really was to her. In fact, she had gotten up half an hour early that morning so she could get to school before homeroom and meet Jeffrey at his locker. She wanted nothing more than to give him a hello kiss and to be reassured that things were still OK.

Elizabeth was waiting for Jeffrey ten minutes before the bell rang for homeroom. She had a note she had written him explaining about how much she loved him, and she knew she'd feel a lot better once she had given it to him.

To her surprise, Jeffrey and Enid walked in through the main door together. They were deep in conversation, and when they saw Elizabeth, both of them looked flustered and slightly guilty. "Hi, Liz!" Jeffrey exclaimed. "What are you doing here so early?"

Enid looked embarrassed. She and Elizabeth had smoothed things over since their disagreement on Friday night, but they hadn't seen very much of each other since. Elizabeth couldn't help thinking her friend was behaving strangely. Why was she acting so weirdly—unless she'd been doing something she didn't want Elizabeth to know about?

"I got here early because I had some stuff to drop off for Mr. Collins," Elizabeth fibbed, slipping the note back into her backpack. She didn't feel like giving it to Jeffrey right then. All of a sudden she felt depressed. She kept hearing Lila's gossip ringing in her head.

Could it possibly be true? Could Enid be trying to steal Jeffrey away from her—even before she had won the scholarship?

*   *   *

By the time Elizabeth got home from school on Wednesday, she was completely miserable. So miserable she wasn't even nervous about Mr. Sterne's arrival the following day. She just felt numb, as if things were slipping out of her control.

She was worried about Enid and Jeffrey, and she had no idea whom to turn to for help.

It seemed that wherever she turned now, the two of them were together. She had bumped into them twice more the previous day—once in the hallway and once in the library—and each time they had greeted her with the same mixture of embarrassment and apprehension, as if they were hiding something.

Enid was really behaving oddly. Elizabeth thought the best way to handle everything would be to sit down and have a real heart-to-heart talk with her friend that very day, knowing that if Enid really *were* feeling something for Jeffrey, she wouldn't be able to hide it. Not from Elizabeth. But when she asked Enid if they could walk home together, Enid had said she had something she needed to work on—in the darkroom! Later that afternoon she and Jeffrey had had plans to go to the beach, but what had happened? He'd broken the date, saying he had promised Enid he would help her with some kind of photo project—in the darkroom. Since when had Enid been so big on photography?

Elizabeth, her eyes stinging, had been about to confront him when Jessica came bounding up. "Lizzie, will you drive the car home? We're having an emergency meeting of the cheerleaders, and Cara wants me to go home with her afterward," she said.

Elizabeth had just sighed. Why not? Now that Jeffrey was going to be busy with Enid, she couldn't walk with Enid or ride with Jeffrey.

She had taken the car keys from her sister without a word. So much for her last day at school before Mr. Sterne arrived to ask everyone about her. She had hoped that she'd really feel bolstered up by her friends, ready for her big interview. Instead she felt about as low as she could imagine!

It was almost four o'clock, and Jessica was hurrying past the tennis courts to the bleachers where Robin Wilson and the rest of the cheerleading squad were waiting. She had been hoping they wouldn't schedule an extra meeting that week—she really wanted to get home and work out the strategy with Steven for the next day. But then she decided that the meeting would be a good chance to fill the other cheerleaders in on the "Sabotage Switzerland" plan. It was absolutely essential that she have some of her friends' help. The important thing was that Mr. Sterne get a bad impression of Elizabeth from enough different people to make him reject her.

"Jessica!" Neil Freemont was waving at her from one of the courts. "Come over here a sec."

Jessica forgot that the other cheerleaders were waiting. Neil, an old friend whom she had dated on and off, was always fun to talk to—especially since he doted on her. Neil was a tall, attractive junior with dark brown hair and nice eyes. She always enjoyed their dates—"fun, but not spontaneous enough" was what she had reported back to Lila and Cara.

She noticed Neil was playing against someone she had never seen before. She certainly would have remembered *that* guy if they had ever been introduced! Tall and fantastically built, he had jet black hair and piercing blue eyes.

"I want you to meet someone," Neil told Jessica. "Jess, this is Kirk Anderson. He just moved here from San Diego. Kirk is trying out for the team."

Jessica put her hand out to shake his. "You haven't started school yet, have you?" she asked curiously. *Because I definitely would have noticed you if you had!* she thought. She couldn't wait to get to practice now and tell everyone the news— there was a new guy at school, and an incredibly handsome one at that!

Kirk frowned. "No. I'm starting next week. I just wanted to make sure I didn't miss the chance to try out for the tennis team. When Neil told

81

me a spot had opened up, I made it my business to be here." He smiled, but it was a cold, arrogant smile. "I didn't want to miss out. After all, I happen to be one of the best tennis players in the state."

Jessica raised her eyebrows. "Oh, really?" she said. *And it looks as if you're really modest, too,* she was thinking.

Kirk nodded. "I intend to turn things around for this team once I've joined," he added. His blue eyes flicked up and down as he inspected Jessica. "So what's the social life like here in Sweet Valley? I bet it's pretty uneventful."

Jessica looked offended. "Sweet Valley isn't so little," she argued. "And the social life happens to be just fine."

"Well," Kirk drawled, "I'm sure with a little work we can get some action going." He gave Jessica a knowing little wink. "Who knows," he added pompously, folding his arms and continuing to look her up and down, "maybe you and I can even get together sometime soon."

Jessica opened her mouth, but before she could tell Kirk what a jerk she thought he was, Neil cut her off. "Kirk has the most amazing serve," he said quickly, looking at him with admiration. "He's really as good as he says he is."

Kirk gave Jessica another wink, and she decided then and there that there was no point in telling him off. The guy was obviously a creep, through and through. As far as she was concerned, Kirk wasn't worth getting to know.

Though it was too bad, she thought as she hurried to cheerleading practice. It wasn't often that such a rotten personality came wrapped in such incredible good looks!

"Liz, are you all right? You seem a little down in the dumps," Mrs. Wakefield observed. The two were in the kitchen, trying to get everything ready for dinner. Steven had just surprised them with a phone call saying he was coming home for a few days and would be there in time to join them for the meal.

"I'm OK—I guess," Elizabeth said flatly, taking the ground beef for hamburgers out of the refrigerator.

"Are you still worried about the impression we're going to make on Mr. Sterne? I think your interview is going to go just fine, honey," Mrs. Wakefield assured her.

"I'm not that worried," Elizabeth said. "I mean, not about Mr. Sterne. I guess all I can do is give this whole thing my best shot and wait and see what happens."

Mrs. Wakefield was quiet for a minute. "Sometimes," she said, "being a mother is a little bit like being a detective. If you're not that worried about Mr. Sterne or the interview, then what are you really worried about?"

"Oh, Mom," Elizabeth said, smiling, "how come you always know when something's bugging me?"

"Call it motherly intuition." Mrs. Wakefield laughed. "You happen to look miserable," she added. "I can see something's really bugging you. Can't you possibly tell me what it is?"

"I guess I can," Elizabeth said. "I'm worried about Jeffrey. I keep getting the feeling . . ." Her voice trailed off uncertainly. "I know this is going to sound really weird, but I think he's already starting to forget about me. And I haven't even gotten admitted to boarding school yet!"

"What gives you the impression he's starting to forget about you? Is he behaving differently?" Mrs. Wakefield demanded.

"Well, yes and no. He's still being the same old sweet Jeffrey every time I see him. But he's not around very much." Elizabeth bit her lip. "He's spending an awful lot of time with Enid," she blurted out.

"Enid? *Your* Enid?"

"Enid Rollins," Elizabeth said patiently. "You know who I mean."

"Yes, but I don't really see . . ." Mrs. Wakefield frowned. "You don't mean that you think Jeffrey's interested in Enid, do you?"

"Why not? It wouldn't be all that strange, Mom. Don't you remember how I met Jeffrey? Enid was madly in love with him. I guess it wouldn't be so unusual for her to start thinking about him again—now that she knows I might be going to boarding school."

Mrs. Wakefield added some salt and pepper to the ground beef. "I see," she said thoughtfully. "And you're basing this assumption on the fact that you've seen them together more often than usual, am I right?"

"Yes," Elizabeth said, her lower lip sticking out just a bit. "They seem to be inseparable the last few days! Every time I see one of them, the other's right behind. They keep mentioning some kind of big photography project Enid needs all sorts of help with."

"Have you asked Enid what it's all about?" Mrs. Wakefield said. "Maybe she really does need help with photography."

"I haven't asked her," Elizabeth admitted. "I don't want to put her on the spot when it's obvious what's going on."

"You mean you don't want to burden yourself with anything like the facts," Mrs. Wakefield said dryly. "Honey, I'm surprised at you. It isn't like you to jump to conclusions. Have you told Jeffrey the way you're feeling?"

"I never even get to see him anymore!" Elizabeth said. "How can I possibly tell him how I'm feeling?"

"Don't you think you're being a little bit unfair to Jeffrey these days?"

Elizabeth stared at her. "What do you mean?" she demanded.

"I mean," Mrs. Wakefield said," that you seem to be asking an awful lot of him. You suddenly announce that what you want more than anything in the whole world is to move to Switzerland for an entire year and study creative writing. The way you put it, Jeffrey would be a real chauvinist if he didn't back you in the whole project. You keep emphasizing how important it will be for *you*—for *your* development, *your* writing, *your* future." She gave the ground beef a vigorous stir. Have you even asked Jeffrey how he feels about the whole thing. It seems to me that you've done an awful lot of assuming for him. You've assumed he's behind your plan. You've assumed he's going to wait around for you. And now you're assuming that he's interested in your best friend! Don't you think it's time you two actually sat down and *talked*?"

Elizabeth blinked. "You're right," she whispered a moment later. "Mom, I can't believe how rotten I've been. He said he didn't want me to go, but I didn't really believe him. I just kind of took it for granted that when he understood how I felt he would be as thrilled as I am about it."

Mrs. Wakefield shook her head. "Honey, this happens all the time. Two people fall in love and the next thing you know, one of them is taking the other one for granted—or they both are. It's probably the greatest challenge a couple faces." She gave Elizabeth a hug. "Talk to him, sweetheart. It's the only thing you can do. Let him know what your worries are, and you can face them together."

Elizabeth's eyes filled with tears. "You're such a wonderful mother," she whispered. "How in the world did you manage to have a klutz like me for a daughter?"

Mrs. Wakefield laughed. "Oh, I don't think you're that bad," she said. "And even if I did think so, I promise I wouldn't let it show—at least as long as Mr. Sterne is around taking notes on your character!"

Elizabeth tried to muster a smile, but she didn't feel very cheerful. She wanted to talk to Jeffrey. And until she did, until she was really able to clear the air, she knew she wouldn't be able to keep her uneasiness from showing.

Nine

"It isn't that we're not glad to see you, Steve," Mrs. Wakefield said, passing him the platter of hamburgers. "We're just curious why you decided to come home in the middle of the week. Is everything all right at school?"

"Oh, it's fine, Mom," Steven said, cramming a roll into his mouth. "Just fine." He winked at Jessica, who pretended not to notice. "Can't a guy just come home every once in a while without a reason? My roommate's parents love it when he drops in!"

"That reminds me," said Jessica. "I met a guy today who looked a lot like your roommate." She sighed. "Too bad he had to be such a creep, because he's *really* cute."

Elizabeth looked around at her family and

sighed. "Jess, you're not going to go on and on about boys in front of Mr. Sterne tomorrow, are you?"

"Boys?" Jessica repeated blankly. "What's she talking about?" she asked the table at large, feigning ignorance. "Liz, are you saying you don't want me to talk about boys tomorrow?"

"Mom," Elizabeth said. "Tell Jessica what I mean."

"Darling, we all know how to behave ourselves," Mrs. Wakefield said.

"I forgot all about Mr. Sterne," Steven said, lying. "What time is he coming?"

"Four o'clock," Elizabeth said, looking nervous just at the thought. "Jess, I was hoping you could wear that navy blue skirt and the flowered shirt Aunt Shirley sent you. You know the one with the little white collar."

Jessica widened her eyes. "You mean that thing that looked straight out of *Peter Pan*? I gave it to the clothing drive at school last month."

"Jess, that wasn't very nice. I'm sure Aunt Shirley spent ages trying to decide what to get you," Mrs. Wakefield said, reproving her.

"I was thinking," Jessica added innocently, "that I might wear that black leather miniskirt and my glittery bandeau and my—"

"Jess!" Elizabeth wailed, covering her face with her hands.

"Can't you see your sister is under pressure?" Steven demanded with mock gravity. "God, Jess, she might crack up if you keep going on this way. For all you know this Mr. Sterne will show up, and Liz will just faint dead away."

"Stop it, both of you," Mrs. Wakefield said. "Liz is going to act just like herself, and I'm sure Mr. Sterne will be suitably impressed. What exactly is your schedule for tomorrow?" she asked Elizabeth.

"I have the interview with him at noon in San Diego, so I'll take the bus down there. I got special permission to leave school. Then he's going to drive me to Palisades, where I'll meet Ms. Crawford, the local alumna, and we'll have a group interview. Then I'll bring Mr. Sterne back to the house so he can meet all of you. Ms. Crawford has a meeting after my interview, so she won't be able to get here until after four o'clock."

"Four o'clock?" Mr. Wakefield stared at her. "Honey, did you tell me about this before? You know I don't get home before six."

"Dad!" Elizabeth shrieked. "He'll think we have a broken family or something."

"Oh, we'll just explain that we all ax-murdered Daddy and buried him in the basement," Jessica said sweetly.

"I'll be here," Mrs. Wakefield said, patting Elizabeth on the hand. "Won't that do?"

From the expression on Elizabeth's face, it was apparent that it wouldn't. "Daddy, I told you about this on Monday," she said. "And you said you could get away early. Don't you remember?"

"I don't. I'm sorry to say, but I guess I can rearrange some of my meetings," Mr. Wakefield said thoughtfully. "I'm really sorry, Liz. Don't worry—I'll manage to get here. And if I'm a few minutes late, just explain to Mr. Sterne that I'm on my way."

Elizabeth stared down at her hamburger. What a family. Steven had arrived out of nowhere—with no real reason for being at home—as if he didn't care about college at all. And her father had managed to forget about Mr. Sterne completely. They were really going to make a great impression!

"Will you excuse me?" she asked, getting to her feet. "I want to try Jeffrey again." His line had been busy before dinner, and by that time she was really anxious to talk to him.

"Go ahead, honey," her mother said. "Jessica and Steven will do the dishes."

Elizabeth hurried out of the room, ignoring the shouts of protest this provoked from her brother and sister. They were behaving like six-year-olds, both of them. God only knew what Mr. Sterne was going to think!

"Mrs. French?" she said several minutes later when the phone had finally been picked up. "It's Elizabeth. Is Jeffrey there?"

"Oh, dear—you just missed him," Mrs. French

said, sounding upset. "I know he'll be disappointed."

Elizabeth glanced down at her watch. "Do you know where he was going?" she asked, trying to hide her disappointment. She really wanted to talk to him badly. She wanted to clear things up and talk about Switzerland—*really* talk—before Mr. Sterne arrived.

"I think he said he was going over to Enid's house," Mrs. French said. "Is that possible? I was on the phone when he was leaving, and I'm not a hundred percent sure, but I think that's where he said he was going."

Elizabeth felt her eyes sting with tears. "Thanks, Mrs. French," she murmured. "I'll talk to him in school tomorrow. Don't bother telling him I called." And before Mrs. French could say any more Elizabeth hung up the phone.

There was no kidding herself any longer. Jeffrey hadn't even waited until she was gone to look for a substitute. Elizabeth just wished he could have chosen someone other than Enid. Because this way she wasn't just losing her boyfriend—she was losing her best friend as well.

"Miss Wakefield? Mr. Sterne is waiting for you," the secretary told Elizabeth the following day. She smiled as Elizabeth crossed the carpeted waiting room and knocked on the door to Mr. Sterne's office. She was really nervous and hoped it didn't show. After a tortured half hour that morning she had selected a gray skirt and a navy blazer to wear, with a pair of flat navy blue shoes. She deliberately left Jeffrey's pin behind. Not that she had seen him that morning anyway. He had left her a good-luck note tucked in her locker, but Elizabeth was certain it was written out of guilt.

But she couldn't think of that because now she had Mr. Sterne to face—and then Ms. Crawford.

"Mr. Sterne? I'm Elizabeth Wakefield," she said after he had gruffly instructed her to come in. Mr. Sterne was younger than she had expected—about her father's age—and was sitting behind a huge glass desk. Everything in his office looked sleek and new to Elizabeth. The only thing on the desk was an open manila file. Elizabeth had the uncomfortable impression her application was in the file.

"It's a pleasure to meet you," she said, trying to sound natural.

Mr. Sterne raised his eyebrows, smiling politely. He had an austere, formal aura that intimidated Elizabeth. "Yes," he said in a high, slightly thin voice. "A pleasure." He gestured to the chair in front of her. "Why don't you have a seat," he said, putting the tips of his fingers together and looking at her as if he were

93

trying to decide then and there what he thought. "Now," he said, after she had sat down, "why don't you tell me about yourself."

Elizabeth took a deep breath. She barely knew where to start. She had the distinct feeling that there was a response Mr. Sterne expected, but she had no idea what that might be. If only he looked a little warmer, a little more receptive! He looked as hard and cold as the glass table in front of him. Still, she had no choice. The chance of winning the Margaret Sterne Memorial Prize rested on this man's approval—and all she could hope was that her natural, relaxed style would win him over! She proceeded to tell him why she wanted to study in Switzerland, particularly at the Interlochen School. "The chance to study with Nadia DeMann means a great deal to me," she added when she had summarized her longing to travel, to learn more about a new culture, and to study under the excellent faculty at the school. "I've always wanted to be a writer. I think working with Nadia DeMann would be the most wonderful thing that could happen to me!"

"Well," Mr. Sterne said, "you certainly seem to have done your research." He smiled, looking a little less frosty than he had when she began. "I appreciate that. It shows how interested you are. Now, you understand how the fellowship works. Your application is being reviewed by Mr. Hummel and the board right now in Geneva. If Ms. Crawford and I agree at the end of our interviewing process, we make both decisions simultaneously. That is, she decides—after talking with Mr. Hummel—whether or not you can be admitted. And I talk to the other members of the Sterne Trust to decide whether or not you receive the fellowship. Does that make sense?" When Elizabeth nodded, he went on, "Of course, for my part I can't emphasize strongly enough how much we'll be looking at your family, your friends, and the way you behave in your natural environment." He smiled encouragingly. "We want to get the opportunity to learn as much about you as we possibly can. So I hope you won't mind if we pay a great deal of attention to you—especially since you seem so very well mannered." He sniffed. "We care so much about *character*—and so few young ladies really exhibit good manners these days!"

Elizabeth breathed an immense sigh of relief.

He put his fingers together again, a gesture Elizabeth was beginning to find worrying. "I'm sure your family must be every bit as *delightful* as you are, though, Miss Wakefield."

Elizabeth managed a weak smile. "Yes," she faltered. "They're—uh, delightful."

She managed to keep smiling as Mr. Sterne got up to signal it was time to move on for the second round of interviews. She hoped everything went smoothly when Mr. Sterne went home with her. He seemed awfully big on this good-manners business. And who could tell whether or not Jessica and Steven could live up to Mr. Sterne's standards?

By four o'clock Elizabeth was exhausted. She'd had no idea how tiring it was to keep smiling, to keep saying the same things over and over again. By the end of the interview with Ms. Crawford, she could barely remember what had seemed so important about studying abroad. But, of course, she didn't let on that her enthusiasm was flagging. She knew she had made a good impression. Even the icy Mr. Sterne seemed to have thawed a little bit, and he actually seemed friendly as they drove to the Wakefields' house together.

"We really do have to keep our standards up," he confided as he pulled his steel gray Mercedes-Benz into the driveway, beaming at the neat split-level ranch home before him. "We can't let just *anyone* represent the Sterne family. It's such a fine old family, you see." He turned off the engine. "I think families reveal so much about character, don't you, Elizabeth?"

"Uh—yes, sir," Elizabeth said, her eyes fastened uncomprehendingly on the motorcycle parked in the driveway. No one in the Wakefield family was allowed on a motorcycle. In fact, Elizabeth had broken this rule once and had been involved in a terrible accident that had only confirmed her parents' unequivocal law: no motorbikes of any kind.

"Gracious," Mr. Sterne said, following her gaze. "Does someone in your family ride that?"

"No," Elizabeth said, her mouth dry. She had no idea what the motorcycle was doing there. She just wished it would disappear!

"This is my brother, Steven," Elizabeth told Mr. Sterne when they got inside, wishing her mother were right there to greet them. She looked more closely at him. It didn't look as though he had shaved that morning! Her heart sinking, she wondered what Mr. Sterne thought. She was sure being unshaven fell under the category of "bad manners." "Steven, where are Mom and Dad?"

"Mom called to say she had an emergency and would be a little late. And you know Dad," Steven added, shrugging.

Elizabeth blinked. "Steven means that my father is always punctual, of course," she said quickly. "But he had a meeting, and he'll be a minute or two late himself."

"We're very relaxed in our attitude toward time, to be honest," Steven remarked to Mr. Sterne. "What's an hour or two when it's sunny outside? That's what my father always says."

"Steven!" Elizabeth exclaimed, horrified. "He never says that!"

"And what do you do?" Mr. Sterne asked

Steven, putting on his glasses and peering down at him.

"Me?" Steven asked. "Oh, I'm a student. I'm in college."

"Ah," Mr. Sterne said. "I see. Are you on vacation now?"

"No," Steven said, yawning a little. "Not really. I just find that I really can't *function* without my family around. See, we're really a tight group—aren't we, Liz—and somehow I just don't seem to be able to *connect* without my family around. We're all that way. We all get lost unless we keep in constant touch. Isn't that true, Liz?"

"I imagine that must make college life rather difficult for you," Mr. Sterne said, looking uncomfortable.

"Oh, yeah. Just ask my professors," Steven said.

Elizabeth was listening to this exchange in horror. She had no idea what to say once it became apparent what Steven was trying to do. "Where's Jessica?" she hissed, fearing the worst was yet to come.

"Poor Jessica," Steven said mournfully. "She just can't stand the thought of losing Elizabeth. See, they're twins—did Liz tell you that? And twins just can't *deal* with being separated. Jessica is totally *unbalanced* about the thought of Liz taking off for your little school in Austria."

98

"Switzerland," Mr. Sterne said, straightening his tie and looking at Steven with alarm.

"Switzerland, Austria, wherever," Steven said pleasantly.

"Excuse me," Mr. Sterne said to Elizabeth. "Can I use your phone for just a minute? I want to let Ms. Crawford know that your parents are going to be a little late. We're all on a very tight schedule, you see."

"Steven, what are you doing?" Elizabeth demanded in a hoarse stage whisper after she had taken Mr. Sterne into her father's study to use the phone. "What's with all this nonsense about our being so dependent on one another? And whose motorcycle is in the front drive? I'm going to kill—"

But she never got a chance to finish her threat. Just then the door opened and Jessica came in, and one look was enough to assure Elizabeth that her chance of winning the Margaret Sterne Memorial Prize was completely finished.

Jessica had actually had the audacity to wear the leather miniskirt. Even worse, she had enough makeup on for Halloween. "Lizzie!" she exclaimed, hurrying over to whirl around for her twin's approval. "Did you see the motorcycle in the driveway? Randy's cousin Tim left it over here. He's coming back in half an hour to pick it up. Isn't it incredible?"

Elizabeth buried her face in her hands. She didn't know what she was dreading more—the argument that was going to break out when her parents saw the motorcycle, or the expression on Mr. Sterne's face when he caught sight of Jessica.

"Hey," she heard a familiar voice exclaim as the front door opened. "Whose motorcycle is out there?"

"Daddy!" Jessica hollered, racing out to the front hall and bumping smack into an astonished—and very unhappy—Mr. Sterne.

"I don't believe we've met," Mr. Sterne said, putting the tips of his fingers together.

"I'm going to die," Elizabeth whispered from the couch. She couldn't believe any of that was happening. All she knew was that she was going to kill them—all of them. She was never going to forgive her family for ruining her chances at the Interlochen School.

Ten

"I couldn't help the way I was dressed," Jessica said, acting hurt. The family had gathered in the living room to discuss what had taken place that afternoon. Elizabeth was livid. She had accused Steven and Jessica of trying to ruin her chances to go to Interlochen on purpose.

Mrs. Wakefield glanced at Jessica's outfit. "You do look a little—extreme, dear," she remarked.

"I happen to have been on my way to a special cheerleading practice," Jessica declared innocently. "We're doing a little routine for the tennis team next week, and we thought we'd do a skit beforehand." She gave Elizabeth a reproachful stare. "I forgot all about Mr. Sterne. Otherwise I would've sneaked out the back door or something."

"And what about the motorcycle?" Elizabeth cried. "Doesn't it seem just a little coincidental, Jess, that you arranged to appear looking as if you're dressed for Halloween *and* Randy's cousin's motorcycle just happened to be parked in our driveway?"

"What motorcycle?" Mrs. Wakefield asked, perturbed. "I thought we'd made our feelings about motorcycles perfectly clear."

"He was only parking it here," Jessica said vaguely, suddenly intent on her manicure.

Elizabeth got to her feet, her eyes filled with tears. "And what about you two?" she demanded, turning to her parents. "Did you have to be late? I told you over and over again how important this was to me. I guess I hoped you'd all come through—and instead you made me look like a real jerk." She glared at Steven. "I don't think I've ever heard anything quite like the stuff *you* came up with! Making us all sound like we can't even leave the room without one another!"

Mr. Wakefield cleared his throat. "I'm sorry, honey," he said softly. "I managed to reschedule my appointment, but I got a last-minute phone call from New York I had to take. I got here as quickly as I could."

Mrs. Wakefield looked upset. "I'm sorry I was late, too. I had to send out some plans for the new building downtown, and I got held up."

Looking stern, Mr. Wakefield turned to Steven and Jessica. "Can you two explain what you were trying to do here? Because if you can't, I'm afraid we're going to have to punish you—and I mean punish severely. You had no business trying to get in the way of your sister's chances for that scholarship, however much you were against it."

"We didn't mean any harm," Jessica objected. "And I don't see what either of us did that was so awful. Mr. Sterne was the terrible one," Jessica pointed out. "What was his problem? He looked like he was from an evil planet on "Star Trek" or something."

Steven giggled. "Jess is right. He kept leering at me. I think the guy's creepy, Liz. Why would you want to go anywhere on a scholarship from his family?"

Elizabeth's face burned. "I still think you were all unfair—every one of you," she cried. "Mr. Sterne was only trying to do his job." She narrowed her eyes. "I just hope the interview tomorrow goes more smoothly. Maybe I can still salvage things. The way it stands now, he just may pity me—he may think I'm a perfectly nice girl who just happens to come from a family of weirdos!"

"That's a fine way to talk," Steven said. "After I tried my hardest to show how loving and concerned we all are."

Elizabeth shook her head. "You're impossible," she said. "To tell you the truth, I don't want to be with any of you. I just want to be alone. Is it OK if I just stay up in my room? I really don't feel much like eating dinner."

Mr. and Mrs. Wakefield exchanged concerned glances. "Sure, honey," Mrs. Wakefield said. "But try not to worry. I'm sure Mr. Sterne couldn't find a better candidate for his prize—even if your family *did* come across as slightly chaotic."

Elizabeth didn't answer. She just felt tired—tired and disappointed. And she had a terrible lump in her throat as she climbed upstairs to mull over all that had just transpired.

"Liz, can I come in?" Mrs. Wakefield asked. It was later that evening, and Elizabeth was sitting at her desk, staring outside unhappily.

"Sure, Mom," she said.

"Jeffrey's on the phone. He says he tried to find you this morning." Mrs. Wakefield came over and patted Elizabeth's shoulder. "He wants to hear how your interview went."

Elizabeth bit her lip, remembering how she felt the night before when she had talked to Mrs. French. "Mom, I can't talk to him right now. Could you tell him I'm asleep?" she asked in a low voice.

Mrs. Wakefield frowned. "Are you sure? He really sounds upset, honey."

Elizabeth took a deep breath. "I'm sure," she said heavily. She couldn't face the thought of talking to Jeffrey, knowing that he was really just counting the minutes until she found out whether or not she'd won the scholarship. She could just imagine what would happen then. At first he'd pretend to be upset. Then little by little he'd show her that he was getting used to the idea. Then—when it became obvious they were going to be separated, that she was really and truly going to boarding school in Switzerland—he and Enid would drop the bombshell.

Elizabeth stared out the window after her mother left the room. How had everything gotten so messed up so quickly? She had been more excited about the Interlochen School than anything she could ever remember. She'd been certain it was the best thing she could possibly do. Now—well, now she really couldn't tell what she was feeling. She couldn't bear the thought of losing Jeffrey. And not just Jeffrey. If she went away, what would happen to her friendships? What about being so far away from Jessica— and her parents?

Elizabeth swallowed. It had all seemed so simple before. Now she didn't know what she wanted—except that she wanted to have a chance at the scholarship. And the way her family had behaved that afternoon seemed to her to have ruined that possibility completely.

If only everything would make sense again! Elizabeth buried her head in her hands. All she could do was hope that she'd impressed Mr. Sterne enough that afternoon to make him ignore Jessica and Steven's behavior.

"How'd you think it went?" Jessica whispered to Steven. They were out on the patio, enjoying the warm evening and rehashing the events of the afternoon. Steven was examining a new cordless telephone Mr. Wakefield had brought home from the office.

"It's hard to say. Sterne seemed so weird it's not easy to figure out what would really bug him the most. But I think we were pretty obnoxious. If only Liz weren't such a perfect candidate!"

Jessica looked at her brother, her blue-green eyes narrowing in thought. "Maybe we should see what we can do about that," she murmured.

"Jess, you have that rotten look on your face," Steven said, laying the telephone down on the patio table. "That conniving, I-think-I'm-going-to-do-something-really-dreadful look that only you can summon up. Don't tell me you've got something up your sleeve."

"You see," Jessica began, thinking out loud,

"it isn't enough making ourselves look rotten. That could backfire. Maybe this Mr. Sterne will go back and tell the committee that Elizabeth's family is completely batty. And then they'll decide she's even better than she is, having managed to be so pulled together despite her weird background. Then they'll give her twice as much money and send her away for twice as long." She looked gloomy. "No, we've got to do something really drastic now. Remember what Mom always says, 'Anything worth doing is worth overdoing.' "

"Spare me," Steven groaned. "Just tell me what you think we should do next."

"OK," Jessica said, lowering her voice. "I think we need to show Mr. Sterne that Liz really isn't the Liz he thinks she is. In other words, she isn't sweet and loyal and helpful. She's actually kind of schizophrenic. She *seems* really great but she's actually boy crazy and unstable, a real basket case."

"Sounds familiar," Steven said fondly, leaning over to rumple Jessica's hair. "Only how do we manage to convince Mr. Sterne?"

"Well," Jessica said thoughtfully, twisting her hair around her finger, "suppose I just *happen* to wear something exactly like what Liz wears to school tomorrow? And suppose I manage to keep bumping into Mr. Sterne—with a different boy each time? And pretend I'm Liz?"

107

Steven's eyes lit up. "Not a bad plan," he said, commending her.

"I'll just have to cut the classes Liz and I have together, but it's worth the risk. After all, I'm saving my own twin sister. Also," Jessica said, leaning forward confidentially, "I heard Liz tell Mom that a big part of the interview is yet to come. Supposedly this Ms. Crawford woman is coming to the school office tomorrow afternoon at two-thirty to meet Mr. Sterne. They'll have one last chance to ask Liz questions—and that's when *you* can help."

"Help? How?"

"Dial the office number and keep asking for Liz. Try using different voices and give different names, so it looks like different guys are trying to reach her. That ought to cinch it!"

"Jess, I don't know what to say." Steven grinned. "I don't know whether to call you a genius or a real jerk."

"How about something in between? Like a devoted, loving twin sister?" Jessica demanded. She leaned forward, grabbing the phone.

"Now what?" Steven asked as she began to dial Lila's number.

"Oh, I just want to make sure everyone else knows what's going on tomorrow." Jessica smiled mischievously. "We're going to need all the help we can get if we're going to undo Liz's fine reputation in a single day!"

*   *   *

"Hey," Mrs. Egbert said, coming into the living room where Winston was sitting alone in the dark, deep in thought. "Are you OK, honey? I thought you'd gone to bed hours ago."

Winston shrugged. "I guess I'm OK. Mom," he said tentatively. "Have you ever had a decision that you just couldn't make? I mean something where you find yourself thinking you're going to do one thing and then the next minute you've completely changed your mind?"

Mrs. Egbert sat down, snapping the lamp on next to the couch. Her face was thoughtful. "Yes," she said after a moment's reflection. "I take it you mean something big—something like a moral dilemma, not just like where to go on vacation or something like that."

"Yeah—a moral dilemma," Winston repeated.

Mrs. Egbert smiled, patting his hand. "I have, honey. More than once. And it never gets any easier to make those kinds of decisions. I guess when it comes right down to it, all you can do is search your soul and ask yourself what you really think is right." She studied him thoughtfully. "Is there any way I can help you?" she asked.

Winston sighed. "I wish you could, Mom. But I guess you're right. This is something I've got to work out for myself."

His mother leaned over to pat his shoulder. "You see how funny life is? I bet most of your

109

friends think you haven't got a care in the world now that you've won the lottery. And here you are looking as though the weight of the world were resting right on your shoulders."

Winston didn't answer. Suddenly he knew that there was only one way to handle his problem. He just couldn't believe it had taken him that long to see what he had to do.

Eleven

Jessica frowned at herself in the full-length mirror inside her closet. *Not bad*, she thought, pivoting a little to inspect the plaid ribbon on her neat blond ponytail. She was dressed exactly the way Elizabeth had been that day, down to the crisp white blouse, the navy blazer, and the pleated gray skirt. Even her shoes and stockings were identical to Elizabeth's. It hadn't been easily arranged, either. Jessica had drafted Steven's help, but he turned out to be completely useless. "What's she wearing?" she had asked when Steven came upstairs from his spying mission at the breakfast table.

"Uh—a skirt. Gray, I think. Or maybe light blue. And a blouse with a pointy collar."

"Some help," Jessica had snapped. The only

solution was to pretend she had overslept—not in itself all that rare an event—and go into Elizabeth's room to wish her good luck. It gave Jessica the chance to inspect her sister herself, to make a mental checklist from the ribbon down to the cream-colored stockings. And as soon as Elizabeth went out to meet Regina, who was driving her to school, Jessica flew into action. Luckily the navy blazers were Christmas presents, and the twins each had one. The gray skirt was harder to duplicate, but Jessica found one at the very back of her closet that was similar enough. The ribbon she had to borrow right from the source, as Jessica had given up ponytails years before. In fact, she felt a little queasy as she studied her reflection. *This had better work*, she thought grimly. *If I have to go around looking like I'm applying for a job as a junior executive, I'd better get some positive results!*

After Steven assured her that the coast was clear—meaning that everyone had left the house—Jessica hurried out to the garage, hopped in the Fiat, and zoomed off for school. It promised to be an interesting day, that was for sure. She had drafted the help of Randy, Neil, and Tom McKay—and she was prepared to improvise by flirting with anyone and everyone she saw—as long as Mr. Sterne was there to witness it!

Jessica didn't come across Elizabeth until the bell had rung after second period. Elizabeth was walking down the hall toward the office, Mr. Sterne beside her in a gray suit. Jessica ducked into an empty classroom, her heart pounding. She couldn't let Mr. Sterne see them together and discover her masquerade. To her relief, Elizabeth shook hands with Mr. Sterne, said something inaudible, and headed down the hallway. Jessica allowed her enough time to fade from view before hurrying after Mr. Sterne, who was on his way to the office.

"Oh, Mr. Sterne!" she sang out sweetly. "I forgot to tell you something."

Mr. Sterne turned around, confused. "I thought you said you were going to class," he said.

"Oh, class," Jessica pooh-poohed. "That can wait. I just realized that I've been forgetting to tell you one of the most important things in my entire life." She batted her eyelashes at him. "Have I mentioned—at all—how very important I think *men* are?"

" 'Men'?" Mr. Sterne repeated blankly.

"You know," Jessica cooed, tucking her arm knowingly through his. "Men."

"No, you haven't mentioned that," Mr. Sterne said, pushing his glasses up and staring at her in consternation.

"Of course I don't believe in limiting oneself," Jessica assured him. "One of my goals is to meet a really rich Swiss banker and spend the rest of my life in luxury. I think it's terribly important for a writer to have some kind of independent means of support, don't you?"

Mr. Sterne gasped. Before he could respond, Randy Lloyd—who had been carefully prepped on what to say and how to act—came hurrying toward them. Jessica hoped he would remember his lines.

"Liz! Darling!" he exclaimed, leaning over to kiss her.

"Randy," Jessica said huskily. "Please meet Mr. Sterne. Mr. Sterne is my friend, Randy." She managed to put as much mysterious emphasis on the word *friend* as possible.

Mr. Sterne shook his head. "I don't understand, Elizabeth," he said primly. "You seem like a completely different young lady from the one with whom I was just—"

"Look! There's Tom!" Jessica gasped, twirling to stare at Tom McKay, a well-built, brown-haired junior who had also been primed on the Sabotage Switzerland Scheme. "I have to dash," she told Mr. Sterne. "Randy, sweetheart, be an angel and walk Mr. Sterne to the office, would you? I have to go ask Tom if he still plans on taking me to the Beach Disco tonight."

" 'Disco'?" Mr. Sterne repeated faintly. But there was no chance for an answer. Randy was hurrying him off to the office, and Jessica was already draping herself all over Tom, her voice half an octave higher than usual as she screeched endearments.

"How's it going?" Tom asked in a whisper when Mr. Sterne was out of earshot.

Jessica gave him a thumbs-up sign. "This is a piece of cake," she assured him and then giggled. "That guy isn't ever going to forgive Liz. And we've only gotten started!"

"Liz," Jeffrey panted, hurrying after her in the hallway. "I've just got to talk to you! Do you realize I've been calling you and chasing after you and trying to find you all over this stupid school for the past couple of days? And you're treating me like an absolute stranger!"

Jessica bit her lip. *Oops*, she thought. Here was something that hadn't occurred to her in advance. "Uh—you know how it is," she said silkily, giving Jeffrey a quick kiss on the cheek. "I've just been so preoccupied ever since I started applying for this scholarship. I'll make it up to you," she promised, her eyes sultry. *I hope Liz appreciates this*, she thought. *Here I am saving her romance. Poor Jeffrey has been totally ignored all week!* "Tonight," she added significantly, giving his arm a squeeze.

Jeffrey stared at her, his mouth dropping open. But before he could say a word, Jessica—her Elizabeth disguise proven now to be a complete success—had dashed off in pursuit of Mr. Sterne, whom she'd just spotted coming out of Mr. Collins's room.

Jeffrey was just going to have to wait!

"Mr. Sterne!" she squealed, slipping her arm through his and steering him toward the student lounge. "I feel that you and I just have *got* to sit down together. Alone," she added meaningfully. "So we can get to know each other better in slightly less *formal* circumstances."

Mr. Sterne disentangled his arm and looked at her with disbelief. "Miss Wakefield," he said, "you are a complete enigma to me. I've just come from talking to Mr. Collins about you, and I have to admit I have never—in all my days of interviewing students for the Margaret Sterne Memorial Prize—heard such a glowing report. It almost took my breath away."

"Mr. Collins is so *darling*, isn't he," Jessica said. Darn, she thought. Here she was doing so well, and Mr. Collins had to complicate everything. "I have to confess I've been madly in love with him ever since I first knew him," she added. "I mean, he's the most gorgeous teacher I've ever seen!"

Mr. Sterne glared at her. "Please!" he snapped. "Remember yourself, young lady! Don't you realize how inappropriate your comments are?"

"Love," Jessica declared passionately, "does not recognize the word *appropriate*, Mr. Sterne." She dropped her eyes as she led him into the student lounge and shut the door. "I would've thought you knew that—being European and everything."

"I'm not European," Mr. Sterne said stiffly. "I happen to represent the family of Miss Margaret Sterne, or have you forgotten?"

"Oh, yes," Jessica said rapturously. "Tell me, Mr. Sterne—what exactly *did* the poor thing die of? I've heard nothing but the nastiest rumors, but of course—"

"Please!" Mr. Sterne snapped, his face turning first pale, then red. "I simply can't bear the thought of anyone spreading rumors about dear, sweet Margaret."

"Sorry," Jessica said. "Oh, dear," she added, glancing down at her watch. "I've *got* to find Tom McKay before this interview of ours. What time is it? Two-fifteen?"

"Yes," Mr. Sterne said coldly. "I do hope you manage to squeeze it into your busy schedule."

"You see, Tom is mad about me," Jessica confided. "But I think I already told you how I feel about Jeffrey. There just isn't room in my life for more than one passionate attachment. Oh, flirtations are another story, of course. But passion . . ." She let her voice trail off as she slipped to the door, smiling knowingly at him.

"I'll see you in a few minutes," she said by way of parting, hurrying through the door before the astonished—and obviously horrified— Mr. Sterne could utter a single word.

*   *   *

117

Elizabeth opened the door to the office at twenty-five minutes past two. She was nervous, but she hoped that Mr. Sterne had heard enough good things about her that day to make the final interview go smoothly.

To her surprise, Mr. Sterne looked unfriendly when she put her hand out to shake his. "Glad you managed to make it on time," he said frostily.

"What do you mean?" Elizabeth asked, astonished. But before he could answer, Ms. Crawford came in. She wasn't smiling.

"We want to tell you, Miss Wakefield, that this is the most confusing case we've ever encountered," Mr. Sterne said, putting the tips of his fingers together. "On the one hand, your file shows you to be a blameless—we might even say a *model*—citizen. You have perfect grades. You've obviously demonstrated concern for your peers and the members of your community in numerous ways. Your teachers have nothing but the highest praise for your work. And your writing samples are truly commendable."

Elizabeth gulped. "That's very kind of you to say, Mr. Sterne, but—"

"*But*"—Mr. Sterne cut her off—"our impression of you so far has only served to confound us. Half the time you seem to behave with the modesty and maturity we might have expected from someone with your credentials. But other times"—he shuddered—"I'm afraid we simply can't put it all together. The parts just don't seem to fit."

Elizabeth stared. "What do you mean?" she demanded.

Just then Rosemary the principal's secretary, knocked on the door. "I'm sorry to interrupt, but there's a phone call for Elizabeth. Someone named John Simmons," she said.

Elizabeth's brow furrowed. "I don't know anyone named John Simmons," she told the secretary. "Can you take a message? Maybe I can get back to him when our meeting is over." She turned back to the two adults, shaking her head. But before she could say another word the secretary was back again.

"John says it's urgent. He says it's about tonight," she told Elizabeth.

Now there was nothing she could do but get up, excuse herself, and answer the phone. By this point Elizabeth was so confused and upset, she didn't know what to think or do. And when she took the phone from the secretary, there was no one on the other line.

"Elizabeth," Mr. Sterne said stiffly when she came back into the room, flustered, "we've decided we need to think this over for the next twenty-four hours. We'll contact you tomorrow afternoon. Thank you very much for your cooperation."

Elizabeth felt tears stinging her eyes. "I feel

119

that there's been some sort of misunderstanding," she blurted out. "I really don't understand how—"

"Yes," Ms. Crawford said coldly. "We all feel a little confused, Miss Wakefield. But you must understand this is a very special scholarship. We can't allow our candidates a single blemish on their characters. And I'm afraid the behavior Mr. Sterne has reported today just cannot be considered acceptable. Unless we can find some way to rectify your record . . ." Her voice hung with a chill in the air.

But Elizabeth didn't say a word. She had been staring dully out the office window, and she had just seen something that made her heart stand still. All of a sudden she had a good idea of what the source of that day's confusion might have been.

She had just seen someone who looked exactly like her, sprinting off toward the parking lot—in a gray skirt, a navy blazer, and wearing a hair ribbon exactly like her own.

Jessica, she thought furiously. She could hardly wait to get her hands on that girl. She was certain of one thing. This was the last trick her twin sister was ever going to play on her—as long as she lived!

Twelve

"I can't believe you two would do something like this to me," Elizabeth cried. She had trapped her brother and sister in the kitchen and was confronting them together. "Every time I think of what it felt like looking out that window and seeing Jessica—dressed exactly like me . . ."

Jessica sighed, looking down at her outfit. "I know what you mean," she said. "It must have been kind of a shock, Liz." She gave Steven an anxious look. "But I still don't think you need to be so hysterical. Who knows what Mr. Sterne and Ms. Crawford will decide?"

"I don't know what you two did, but I know you did something," Elizabeth said, brushing away her tears. "And I want to hear the entire thing. From the beginning."

Steven looked uncomfortable. "Maybe we were kind of wrong," he said reluctantly. "But you've got to believe us, Liz. It was only because we didn't want you wrecking your life, going off to some snobby boarding school. We really did what we did out of—you know, out of family loyalty."

Stony faced, Elizabeth crossed her arms. "I want to know," she repeated grimly, "exactly what you two did. Jessica, let's start with what you said to Mr. Sterne today to give him the impression that I'm some kind of raving lunatic."

Jessica's eyes widened innocently. "Lunatic? Is that what he said?" she demanded.

"No, that isn't what he said," Elizabeth said, seething. "But it's what he implied. Come on, Jessica. You can't stand there wearing an outfit exactly like mine and tell me that you weren't sneaking around today pretending to be me."

"I did *not* sneak," Jessica retorted hotly. "I may have pretended to be you, but I never sneaked!"

"Jessica," Elizabeth said, grabbing hold of the counter as if to steady herself, "I'm going to count to ten, and when I'm done counting I want an explanation. Do you hear me?"

Jessica took a deep breath. She'd seen her twin angry before, but this was something new. "I—uh, well, Steven and I thought—that is—"

"Let's face it, Jess. We owe Liz an apology," Steven said unhappily. "But, Liz, we really did mean well. We felt that you'd just kind of lost it about going to Switzerland. We tried talking you out of it, but that didn't work. So we figured we'd try to keep you from going by something a little more indirect."

Elizabeth's lower lip quivered. "I don't suppose it occurred to either one of you that the reason that you couldn't talk me out of it was because I really wanted to go," she said shakily. "I happen to have had a dream that could have come true, and you two managed to ruin it for me."

Jessica looked distraught. The one thing in the world she couldn't stand was seeing her twin upset. Suddenly she felt filled with shame for the things she and Steven had done. "Liz, we were jerks," she said, putting her arms around her. "Can you ever forgive us?"

Elizabeth pulled away from her, her tears spilling over. "No," she said sharply. "I can't. I know you two may have thought this would end up being funny, but the truth is I think what you did today was really, really rotten. I still don't know the details, but I can guess what must have happened. Jessica, you pretended to be me in front of Mr. Sterne, right? Only instead of being *me*—the real me—you said a bunch of awful things and made me look like a prize idiot. And you"—she turned to her brother with a look of incrimination in her eyes—

"you probably were behind that phone call that wrecked my last interview this afternoon."

Jessica and Steven hung their heads. "But remember, it was only because we wanted to keep you here in Sweet Valley!" Jessica burst out.

"I don't care what your reason was," Elizabeth said, her face flushed. "It was despicable. I thought my family was behind me. And I've learned the hard way that I was wrong!" With that Elizabeth spun on her heel and raced from the room, slamming the door behind her.

"Wow," Steven said dully, staring down at the floor. "I feel like a criminal."

"Me, too," Jessica said sorrowfully. "Steve, how could you possibly have convinced me to do such a terrible thing?"

"*Me*—convince *you*?" Steven repeated incredulously. "Jessica, how dare you! You know dressing up like Liz was your idea."

"Yeah, but what about acting like dopes around Mr. Sterne yesterday? Whose idea was that?" Jessica reminded him.

Steven glared at her. "For your information, Miss High and Mighty, it so happens—"

"Steven, listen to me," Jessica interrupted, the expression in her eyes thoughtful. "Does it really matter whose idea it was?"

"I guess not," Steven admitted. "Elizabeth is all that matters. I just wish there was something we could do to make it up to her."

"I know," Jessica said, biting her lip. She was

124

really worried. She couldn't remember ever having seen Elizabeth so upset, and she knew they were going to have to do something to reestablish trust. Having Elizabeth despise her was even worst than having her go off to boarding school in Switzerland!

"I've got an idea," Jessica said suddenly. "Look, we got Elizabeth into this whole mess by trying to make her appear to be something she isn't to Mr. Sterne and the committee. Why don't we call him and make an appointment to see him? We can tell him the truth—from the beginning. At least that way he'll know Liz is really everything her teachers and her records say she is. Then maybe she'll forgive us."

"Yeah," Steven said unhappily. "But then won't they turn around and give her the scholarship after all?"

Jessica shrugged. "There isn't much we can do about that," she told him. "Liz is right, Steve. We really have to let her make up her own mind."

But even as she spoke she felt a pang of remorse. Confessing the truth to Mr. Sterne would be about the hardest thing she had ever done in her whole life!

After Elizabeth had run out of the room, she dashed upstairs, threw herself on her bed, and cried herself to sleep. She rested fitfully, having snatches of disturbing dreams that she could only half remember when she woke up at five o'clock. The house was quiet, and she felt terrible, her mouth dry and her head throbbing. Everything came flooding back to her, and she felt even worse. Maybe going for a jog along the ocean would clear her head, she thought. She changed into a pair of shorts and a T-shirt, and as she reached for her running shoes her gaze fell on the tiny pearl pin Jeffrey had given her. She stopped to pick it up, her eyes thoughtful. How had everything become so terribly confused? It felt like days since she and Jeffrey had even spoken. She decided to jog past his house on the way to the beach. If his car was in the driveway, she would go in and talk to him—maybe see what he was doing that night.

She had to admit it felt good to get some exercise. Her anger at Jessica and Steven faded a little bit as she began to warm up, jogging leisurely along the tree-lined streets down toward the beach. OK, so they had acted irresponsibly—even immorally. But hadn't they behaved the way they did out of love, however misguided? She supposed it might be worse if neither of them even cared what she did.

And the truth was that her own feelings about Mr. Sterne were deeply ambivalent. She hadn't liked him very much. She had found him tense, difficult to talk to, and too pretentious. She didn't like the way he had interrogated her family, either.

And she also had to admit she had been having serious misgivings about the Interlochen School. What had appealed to her so much had been largely a fantasy—the image of a perfect chalet nestled among fir trees in the Alps and the dedicated teachers and aspiring students. She hadn't actually bothered to think about what day-to-day life would be like thousands of miles from her friends and family. Yes, she would no doubt receive a wonderful education, but at what cost? Wouldn't she be giving up an awful lot by leaving Sweet Valley?

Elizabeth slowed down as she reached the Spanish-style house where the Frenches lived. She stopped to catch her breath and wipe her brow before heading down the steep drive to the front door. Then she saw the Rollinses' familiar blue sedan in the driveway and froze. What was that car doing there, unless . . . The next minute she saw Enid, deep in animated conversation with Jeffrey. They were standing close together, and Enid had one hand on his arm, gesturing with the other.

Elizabeth caught her breath in a half gasp, half sob. This was it—the final straw. She was too late. She may have decided just then that the Interlochen School and the Margaret Sterne Memorial Prize weren't for her. But Jeffrey had clearly decided that he couldn't wait around for her to make up her mind. And Enid didn't seem to remember her best friend, either.

Well, Eilzabeth didn't see any reason to break up their newfound happiness. Taking slow, deliberate breaths to keep from crying, she walked rapidly past the driveway, and then broke back into a jog.

There was no reason to stop after all.

Winston shifted his weight from one foot to the other, waiting for Mr. Oliver to come to the door. It seemed to take ages, but at last the old man appeared, his gait shuffling.

"Why, hello, young man!" Mr. Oliver exclaimed. "Please come in! I've been wondering how you were, as a matter of fact."

Winston looked quickly around him, swallowed, and took a deep breath. "Mr. Oliver, what I'm going to say may sound kind of strange. Will you promise not to be too disappointed in me if I tell you that I've done you a really bad turn?"

Mr. Oliver looked upset. "I can't imagine a fine young man like you ever doing anyone a bad turn," he objected.

Winston sighed, pulling his original lottery ticket out of his pocket. "See this?" he said, handing it to Mr. Oliver.

Mr. Oliver studied it for a moment. "Looks like a lottery ticket," he said cheerfully, handing it back to Winston. "I hope you have better luck with it than I ever have! I said I would stop buying the darned things, but I just can't break the habit." He smiled good-naturedly. "Maybe one of these days I'll get lucky."

"That's the whole point, Mr. Oliver," Winston said, looking anguished. "This ticket is mine. *Yours* is at the state lottery office. Remember when we got our jackets mixed up?"

"Of course. That's how we met in the first place," Mr. Oliver said, looking confused.

"Well, this ticket was in my jacket. And the other ticket was in yours."

"That's all right, son. The darned things are all the same," Mr. Oliver assured him, patting him on the back.

"No, they're not," Winston blurted out. "Your ticket actually won. It's worth twenty-five thousand dollars! I went back to the state lottery office and explained to them what happened. When you come in, they'll give you the money they'd given to me."

Mr. Oliver stared at him uncomprehendingly. "You mean—"

"It won. It actually won," Winston told him.

Mr. Oliver sank down into a chair, burying his face in his hands. "I don't believe it," he whispered.

"Please forgive me for taking so long to bring it back to you," Winston begged him. "The thing is, I knew the money really belonged to you. But I just couldn't make myself give it up at first. It was like a dream come true, you know? I'd always wondered what it would be like to have lots of money. So I fooled myself into thinking that I could keep it." He hung his head. "I owe you an apology. I should have brought you the ticket the minute I found out it was a winner."

Mr. Oliver wiped the corners of his eyes. "To think—you say I've won twenty-five thousand dollars?" he repeated in a hoarse voice. When Winston nodded, he went on, "I'll be able to send little Lisa to camp. And I can help her parents, too—they need to get their car repaired. And I can make sure her Christmas this year is really special." Trembling with excitement, he got to his feet. "Son, what you've done today took more courage than if you'd given the ticket back the night you won. You could easily have kept it. It takes real courage to own up to something like this." He wiped his eyes again. "In my book you're the greatest hero that ever lived. And I want to tell the people at the lottery that, too."

Winston felt a lump forming in his throat. He looked down at the floor, embarrassed. "I still should've come sooner," he muttered. "I wanted to. I sent Lisa a doll—did she get it?"

"You sent that?" Mr. Oliver said delightedly. "Son, you made her the happiest little girl in

California! You should've heard her the day it came. It hasn't been out of her arms since!''

Winston was pleased. "So, you will forgive me?" he asked weakly. "You don't think I'm a crook, trying to steal your ticket?"

"Are you kidding?" Mr. Oliver demanded. "I don't know how I can make it any clearer. I think you're the finest young man I've ever met." He put his arms out, and Winston, still hanging his head, crept forward to receive his hug.

His eyes filled then. He knew he had done the right thing. And he wouldn't have traded the feeling he had right then in Mr. Oliver's arms for ten times the amount that lottery ticket was worth!

Thirteen

When Elizabeth got back from jogging she felt
as if her whole world had crashed in on her.
Her parents had been home, but Elizabeth only
said hello to them. Jessica and Steven were out
somewhere. And it suddenly seemed to Elizabeth that things were as bad as they could possibly be. Her chance of attending the Interlochen
School had been completely destroyed; Mr.
Sterne probably thought she was insane, acting
one way half the time and another way the
other half; and worst of all, she had managed to
lose not only her best friend, but her boyfriend
as well. While she was taking a shower, she
heard the front door slam, and she assumed
either Jessica or Steven or both had come home.
She could hardly wait to yell at them again.

"I can't believe you could have done this to me!" Elizabeth screamed, having found Jessica and Steven in the living room after she had dried off and gotten dressed. "Do you have any idea how much it meant to me to be able to try for that scholarship? And now look what's happened!"

Jessica's eyes filled with indignant tears. "I was only trying to help," she protested.

"I want to know what's going on here," Mr. Wakefield said, walking into the room. "Would someone explain this to me, or am I supposed to figure it out while you two scream at each other?"

"We were wrong," Steven said to Elizabeth, crossing his arms in front of his chest. "But did it ever occur to you that we did what we did because we love you so much?"

"I want to know exactly what you did," Mrs. Wakefield exclaimed.

Just then Prince Albert, the Wakefields' tan Labrador retriever puppy, began to bark and jump up and down. The doorbell rang, and the living room truly seemed to be in a state of chaos.

"I want everyone to stop yelling for just one minute!" Mr. Wakefield cried, holding up his hands. "I'm going to answer the door," he told them all, fighting for calm. "And when I come back with whomever is there, I'm going to ask you to explain—very calmly, and *one at a time*—

exactly what has been going on around here. Is that perfectly clear?"

"It's perfectly clear, dear," Mrs. Wakefield told him as the doorbell rang again. "Now don't you think you should go get the door?"

Elizabeth took a long, shuddering breath. "Mom, you should've seen the look on Mr. Sterne's face," she said. "The whole thing was like a nightmare! And then Rosemary came in saying someone named John Simon was on the phone—"

"Simmons. John Simmons," Steven corrected patiently.

"Who cares?" Elizabeth snapped. "The point is—"

"The point is, you all need to stop shouting," Mrs. Wakefield said wearily. "Remember, your parents have had a long, hard week. It's Friday night, and I think both your father and I would really like to sit down and put our feet up. Then, and only then, we're going to hear what happened with Mr. Sterne today."

Elizabeth's eyes flew open. "Oh, no—Mr. Sterne!" she exclaimed, staring as her father came back into the living room accompanied not only by Mr. Sterne, but by Ms. Crawford as well. Elizabeth felt faint. What on earth were they doing here? And she wasn't even dressed up or anything. She looked down in dismay at her jeans and crewneck sweater.

Ms. Crawford was introduced, and Mr. Sterne

—looking as stiff as ever in the same impeccable gray suit—approached the chair that was offered him, then seemed to reconsider and remained standing. "I'm not going to keep you all for long," he announced, polite as ever. "I'm here under what I think are highly unusual circumstances. Ordinarily we don't pay an unannounced visit. But I think there's been some confusion that we'd like to clear up."

"Oh, dear," Mrs. Wakefield said, staring around the room. "Exactly what happened?"

No one said anything for a long, uncomfortable moment. Then Mr. Sterne, clearing his throat and putting the tips of his fingers together, resumed. "We all got a little confused today during the interviewing process. Suffice it to say that we jumped to some pretty harsh conclusions about Elizabeth, here—mostly because of the efforts of her brother and sister."

"Steven! Jessica! How could you?" Mrs. Wakefield said.

Mr. Sterne raised one narrow hand. "Please," he said, "do let me finish."

Mr. and Mrs. Wakefield exchanged amused smiles. Something about Mr. Sterne's manner made them feel as if they were being reproached by an angry teacher. "I don't think I've ever encountered a case like this one," he continued. "Ms. Crawford and I were all set to close Elizabeth's case this afternoon. We felt that she had promise as a writer, exceptional grades and recommendations, but her behavior seemed to us erratic—in fact, wildly so. Then we learned that this was facilitated by her twin's having disguised herself as Elizabeth in order to give us as bad an impression as possible."

"Jessica Wakefield—" Mr. Wakefield began, his expression harsh.

"We learned this," Mr. Sterne continued, "when Jessica and Steven called my office late this afternoon to confess what they had done."

Now it was Elizabeth's turn to look astonished. "You're kidding!" she said out loud. Mr. Sterne looked at her, raising his eyebrows.

"Are you surprised?" he asked her. "It so happens that your brother and sister love you so much, Miss Wakefield, that they were willing to try anything—even the kind of perverse behavior we saw over the course of the past twenty-four hours—to keep you from leaving home." He smiled at Ms. Crawford, who was beaming. "Now, Ms. Crawford and I have agreed, after much discussion, that this in itself speaks very highly of your character. And thanks to the impassioned case that Steven and Jessica have made, we've decided to offer you the Margaret Sterne Memorial Prize. Ms. Crawford is here representing the Interlochen School. There will still be formalities, of course, but once the scholarship is assured you'll receive official notice of your acceptance from Mr. Hummel."

A hush fell over the room. Elizabeth stared

first at Jessica, then at Steven, her lips trembling. "I can't believe you two," she cried, running over at last and hugging them both at the same time.

The next minute the doorbell rang. "Not again!" Mrs. Wakefield cried, jumping to her feet. "It's beginning to feel like Grand Central Station in here," she added, stepping over the yelping Prince Albert.

Elizabeth took the hand Mr. Sterne extended and shook it uncertainly. "I—uh, thank you," she stammered. "I barely know what to say."

"Of course we'll give you the weekend to think it over," he said, looking as if there were no question at all as to what her decision would be.

Elizabeth was about to respond when she looked up and saw Enid and Jeffrey in the doorway of the living room. The words caught in her throat, and she stood absolutely frozen, staring at them. They entered the room, both staring at her.

"Will you excuse me?" Elizabeth managed to say, turning to Mr. Sterne and Ms. Crawford. "I—uh, these are my friends, and I think we need to say a few things to one another."

"Of course," Ms. Crawford said as Elizabeth crossed to her friends.

"Liz," Enid said, all choked up, "we've been spending every spare minute this week working on this for you. It was supposed to be a

137

good-luck present, but from what your mom just told us, it sounds like it'll be a going-away present, too." She handed Elizabeth a beautiful leather scrapbook. "It's to make sure you don't forget about us," she whispered.

Elizabeth stared down at the scrapbook. With trembling fingers she turned the pages. The pictures inside were beautifully arranged, each representing a wonderful memory: one of her playing at the beach with Enid, another with Jessica; dancing with Jeffrey; skiing with her friends; playing tennis on the Patmans' tennis courts; eating lunch at the tables outside the school. The last few pages were filled with pictures of Elizabeth with Jeffrey, and her eyes stung as she turned the pages.

"You mean—all this week you were working on this?" she choked out. "Every time I saw you together?"

"We wanted it to be a surprise," Enid said anxiously, coming forward to put her arm around Elizabeth. "I felt like such a jerk after the way I acted last week. You know how I feel about you, Liz. And if you want to go to Switzerland, I'm behind you one hundred percent."

"Hey," Jeffrey said gruffly, leaning over to kiss her on the cheek, "don't you and I have a date tonight?"

"Whoops," Jessica said, clapping her hand over her mouth. "Jeffrey, we kind of got our wires crossed. That was me this afternoon, not Liz."

Jeffrey stared from Jessica to Elizabeth. "Wait a minute. I think I'm missing something important here." He looked around at everyone in the room, perplexed. "Can someone fill me in, or is it too late?"

"Jeffrey," Elizabeth said suddenly, grabbing his hand, "I need to talk to you." She turned to Mr. Sterne. "Would you mind? I really need to be alone with him for a little while."

"Please," Mr. Sterne said, slightly stiffly. "Do as you must."

"Go ahead, sweetheart. We'll be right here when you get back," her mother said quickly.

Elizabeth felt her heart begin to pound. She couldn't believe this was really happening. It looked as though she had gotten the whole thing wrong, from the very beginning. And now it was time to get it right!

Elizabeth and Jeffrey were sitting out on the Wakefields' front porch, their hands locked tightly. "What I can't believe," Jeffrey said softly, "is that you never told me what you were thinking. You mean to say you honestly believed there was something going on between Enid and me?"

Elizabeth nodded. "I know it sounds crazy now, but I did. I kept seeing you two together.

139

I thought"—she gulped—"I thought you were trying to forget me because I was going to go away."

Jeffrey leaned over and cupped her chin with his hand. "Listen to me," he said fiercely. "Nothing in the whole world is going to make me forget about you, you hear me? Not if you tell me you're leaving for Switzerland tomorrow. I'm not losing you, Liz. I love you too much for that."

"Oh, Jeffrey," Elizabeth said, her voice shaking. She put her head on his shoulder, her eyes welling up with tears.

"I'm really proud of you for winning that prize," Jeffrey continued. "I guess I always knew you could do it, but I'm proud of you, anyway. And you know something? If you decide to go, I'll really understand. I'm not going to forget you, no matter what. So don't let that influence you when you make up your mind."

Elizabeth grabbed his hand. "Come on," she said, pulling him to his feet. "I've made up my mind. In fact, it's been made up all along. I just never realized it until right this minute."

Jeffrey stared searchingly at her.

"Let's go inside," Elizabeth murmured. "I think we've kept them all waiting long enough."

"This isn't going to be very easy for me to say," Elizabeth told the group assembled in the

140

living room. "You've all been very patient with me for the past few weeks. And I guess I owe every single person in this room a big thank-you." Her eyes shone as she turned to Enid. "First, I want to thank Enid for reminding me what a real friend is. I guess a friend is always a reminder of home. And that's what Enid is to me. Her present is an example of that. She's part of what I love most about Sweet Valley."

She turned to her family then, her eyes moist. "I don't think I have to tell Jessica and Steven how angry I was at them this afternoon. But what they did also made me feel good. They weren't going to let me leave without a struggle—and even if they embarrassed me more than a little, it was worth it in the end, especially since they made it all turn out OK."

She sighed and turned to Mr. Sterne and Ms. Crawford. "And most of all I want to thank you for your time and patience. You have generously chosen me to represent Margaret Sterne with your scholarship." She took a deep breath. "But I'm sorry to tell you that I can't accept."

A silence fell across the room.

"Can't accept!" Mr. Sterne exclaimed, astonished. "Do you realize that no one has ever turned down this scholarship offer before? Not in twenty years?"

Elizabeth smiled, shaking her head. "I can believe that. The scholarship is very generous, and the Interlochen School looks like a wonderful place to study." She looked seriously around the room. "It's just that I belong here, with my family and friends. I thought Switzerland was the most magical place on earth, but I can see now that this"—she spread out her arms—"is even more magical. I was looking for inspiration, and I discovered it's right here—with the people who love me most."

Ms. Crawford began to clap. Then Mr. Wakefield joined in, and Steven, and soon the entire room was filled with applause. Even Mr. Sterne looked a little less severe than usual as he leaned over to shake Elizabeth's hand.

"Well, we certainly respect your decision," he said, clearing his throat.

Elizabeth thanked him, but her eyes were intent on Jeffrey's.

"Hey," he said gruffly, putting his arms around her and kissing the top of her head, "welcome home, Liz."

Elizabeth tightened her arms around him, her eyes filling with tears. She didn't know whether she felt like laughing or crying. She just knew she had made the right decision.

This was where she belonged—where the magic and inspiration really were. And she would never forget that again!

Fourteen

"I can't believe it!" Jessica shrieked, opening the newspaper and spotting a large picture of Winston. "Lila, listen to this: 'Lottery Winner Claims He Is Not Rightful Owner of Winning Ticket.' And the subtitle says, 'Generous Boy Proclaimed a Hero by Owner.'"

Lila yawned. She and Jessica were sitting out on the lawn in front of school, waiting for school to begin. "Let me see," she said after she had made sure Jessica wouldn't mistake her interest for enthusiasm. She peered over Jessica's shoulder. Sure enough, there was Winston, grinning in his usual lopsided fashion at the camera.

"Wow," Jessica said, reading quickly. "Can you believe it? Winston gave this guy back a ticket worth twenty-five thousand dollars." She shook her head, her blond hair flying. "I'm not sure I would've done it."

"I certainly wouldn't have," Lila said, looking disgusted. "How is that boy ever going to get anywhere with that kind of confused value system?" She wrinkled her nose. "I should have my daddy send him to one of his cutthroat business seminars. That would teach him not to throw out twenty-five thousand dollars." She pouted. "Besides, I thought he was going to buy us all presents and stuff. Now what are we going to get out of the whole thing?"

"Look—here comes the local hero now," Jessica said, putting down the paper. Winston was heading up the front walk, his arm around Maria and a big smile on his face.

"Winston," Jessica called, "is the story about you for real? Did you really give away twenty-five thousand dollars just because you got your ticket confused with some old man's?"

"You have heard of my valor," Winston declared with mock ceremony. "You see, Maria, my reputation precedes me." He grinned. "From now on, consider me the Moral King of Sweet Valley High. For a modest fee I'll be happy to offer counsel on the thorniest questions. First there was Socrates—then Plato—and now Winston Egbert."

Lila groaned. "Try not to make us sick, Winston," she said. "We can't decide whether or not to have you committed. You're trying to tell us you handed this old man twenty-five thousand bucks?"

"Maria," Winston said grandly, "tell them the sordid facts."

"He really did give back the money," Maria said. I couldn't believe it at first, either." She gave Winston's arm a squeeze. "But I am proud of him. You should see how happy Mr. Oliver is. He's practically adopted Winston!"

"In fact," Winston said, still smiling, "he and I are going to give a party together next weekend on the beach. We're inviting all our friends, and Mr. Oliver's using some of the lottery money to throw it. You ought to see him," he added. "He's so excited about being able to give a party for the first time. And the best part for him will be when he gives his granddaughter the news that he's going to be able to send her to riding camp this summer."

"You could've thought a little bit more about the rest of us, Winston," Lila said, pursing her lips. "I don't think it was very considerate of you just to hand in the cash without buying one of us a single present."

Winston grinned. "I'll try to make it up to you, Lila. I don't know how, but I'm sure I'll be able to think of some way."

And with that he walked off, still holding Maria's hand.

145

"Some people," Lila said, shaking her head.

Jessica nodded, her eyes intent on the other side of the lawn where Kirk Anderson and Neil Freemount were approaching the building. It was Kirk's first day in school and already he was acting as though he owned the place. That Kirk, she thought. He looked at every girl as if he were expecting her to drop dead from excitement or something. Jessica couldn't understand how anyone could be so arrogant. She made a mental note to say something to Neil about Kirk later on.

But for then she had other things to do—like getting Lila inside before the bell rang, so they'd have time to go to the girls' room and make sure they looked OK before classes started.

"Thank goodness you didn't accept that scholarship, Liz," Penny Ayala remarked. Penny, the editor-in-chief of *The Oracle*, was eating lunch with Elizabeth that Monday, and somehow the topic had turned to the paper's general performance. Elizabeth, Penny, and Olivia Davidson, the arts editor, were brainstorming to see if they could think of a good new feature to add to the paper.

"Actually," Penny said thoughtfully, "Lynne Henry had a wonderful idea. We were talking about *The Oracle* this weekend at the beach, and she suggested a personals column. Do you think that might work?"

Elizabeth's eyes brightened. "That's a fantastic idea!" she exclaimed. She really liked Lynne, a tall, auburn-haired girl with striking eyes who had won schoolwide acclaim when her entry in The Droids' songwriting contest was declared the winner. "Lynne is really creative," Elizabeth added, impressed. "A personals column would be terrific. Just think how much attention the paper would get!"

"Look, there's Lynne now. Let's call her over," Penny suggested.

A few minutes later everyone seemed to have suggestions for how the column could work.

Lynne looked thoughtful. "What I was thinking about," she said slowly, "was getting people to submit little blurbs, like 'Cute junior, blond, blue eyes, wants to meet same with interests in biking and guitar.' Things like that."

"We could set up boxes here in the office," Elizabeth suggested. "We could put a number on each of them. Each ad would include a box number, and responses would have to come by letter to the box."

"Hmm," Penny said, looking interested. "And since people would be writing the ads themselves, all we'd really need is someone to coordinate them—to edit them first and just take care of layouts."

Elizabeth and Olivia exchanged glances. Both were very busy with the paper as it was.

"Lynne," Penny said slowly, "I know you're not on the staff of the paper, but since it was your idea, how would you like to be the one to edit the column?"

"I'd like that," Lynne said, smiling shyly. "If you think I can do it, that is."

"Lynne Henry, you're on," Penny declared, jumping to her feet. "Our brand-new personals ads will be coordinated by the hit songwriter Lynne Henry! What a coup!"

Elizabeth and Olivia burst into applause. "See," Olivia said, leaning closer to Elizabeth with a grin, "aren't you glad you didn't let those people drag you off to Switzerland? This is going to be one feature you wouldn't want to miss for the entire world!"

By the end of that week, *The Oracle* was announcing its new column. Posters were up in front of the office and on the bulletin boards in the library, the student lounge, and the cafeteria. "Dateless? Mateless?" they said in big letters. "Don't be sad—run an ad! Just pick up a form from *The Oracle* office and look for love the modern way!"

"Wow," Jessica said, looking at a poster over Cara's shoulder. "I can't believe how progressive *The Oracle* is getting. Seems a little iffy to me, though."

"I don't know," Cara said. "Maybe it's a good idea. Just think of the lonesome people out there who really want to meet someone. Why not use an ad?"

Jessica tossed her hair. "I've always felt bad for people who had to run ads for something perfectly simple—like dating," she said. "Don't you think it looks a little bit desperate?"

Cara shook her head. "I don't think so. I think *The Oracle* is doing people a real service."

Jessica giggled. "Maybe. I'm just glad I'm not one of those poor souls who needs to advertise myself in print!"

Lila, who had just come up to join them, scanned the poster with interest. "I think this is tragic," she announced. "What's the world coming to, anyway? Doesn't anyone believe in passion and romance anymore?" She sniffed. "I'm glad *I* would never have to resort to something like this," she added.

"Better not let Winston advertise." Jessica giggled. "He'd probably get a response from Brooke Shields and then give her back, claiming he'd gotten the wrong person's date."

Lila leaned closer to inspect the poster. "Do you really think it will work?" she asked. "Who's going to come right out and admit he can't get a date on his own?"

Jessica and Cara exchanged glances. Jessica couldn't help agreeing with Lila in principle. On the other hand, who could say what the response from their classmates would be?

Only one thing was certain: with the first personals column coming in a short time, things were certainly going to get exciting at Sweet Valley High!

What couples will find true love through The Oracle's *new personals column? Find out in Sweet Valley High #39,* **SECRET ADMIRER.**

☐ 26682	**RUNAWAY #21**	$2.75
☐ 26745	**TOO MUCH IN LOVE #22**	$2.75
☐ 26689	**SAY GOODBYE #23**	$2.75
☐ 26684	**MEMORIES #24**	$2.75
☐ 26748	**NOWHERE TO RUN #25**	$2.75
☐ 26749	**HOSTAGE! #26**	$2.75
☐ 26750	**LOVESTRUCK #27**	$2.75
☐ 26825	**ALONE IN THE CROWD #28**	$2.75
☐ 25728	**BITTER RIVALS #29**	$2.50
☐ 25816	**JEALOUSY LIES #30**	$2.50
☐ 25886	**TAKING SIDES #31**	$2.75
☐ 26113	**THE NEW JESSICA #32**	$2.75
☐ 26198	**STARTING OVER #33**	$2.75
☐ 26294	**FORBIDDEN LOVE #34**	$2.75
☐ 26341	**OUT OF CONTROL #35**	$2.75
☐ 26478	**LAST CHANCE #36**	$2.75
☐ 26530	**RUMORS #37**	$2.75
☐ 26568	**LEAVING HOME #38**	$2.75
☐ 26673	**SECRET ADMIRER #39**	$2.75
☐ 26703	**ON THE EDGE #40**	$2.75
☐ 26866	**OUTCAST #41**	$2.75
☐ 26951	**CAUGHT IN THE MIDDLE #42**	$2.95
☐ 27006	**HARD CHOICES #43**	$2.95

Prices and availability subject to change without notice.

Buy them at your local bookstore or use this page to order.

- -

Bantam Books, Dept. SVH2, 414 East Golf Road, Des Plaines, IL 60016

Please send me the books I have checked above. I am enclosing $_____
(please add $2.00 to cover postage and handling). Send check or money order
—no cash or C.O.D.s please.

Mr/Ms _____

Address _____

City/State _____ Zip _____

SVH2—6/88
Please allow four to six weeks for delivery. This offer expires 8/88.

EXCITING NEWS FOR ROMANCE READERS

Loveletters—the all new, hot-off-the-press Romance Newsletter. Now you can be the first to know:

What's Coming Up:
* Exciting offers
* New romance series on the way

What's Going Down:
* The latest gossip about the SWEET VALLEY HIGH gang
* Who's in love . . . and who's not
* What Loveletters fans are saying.

Who's New:
* Be on the inside track for upcoming titles

If you don't already receive Loveletters, fill out this coupon, mail it in, and you will receive Loveletters several times a year. Loveletters . . . you're going to love it!

Please send me my free copy of Loveletters

Name _____ Date of Birth _____

Address _____

City _____ State _____ Zip _____

To: LOVELETTERS
BANTAM BOOKS
PO BOX 1005
SOUTH HOLLAND, IL 60473

BANTAM
SHOP·AT·HOME
C·A·T·A·L·O·G

Special Offer
Buy a Bantam Book
for only 50¢.

Now you can order the exciting books you've been wanting to read straight from Bantam's latest catalog of hundreds of titles. *And* this special offer gives you the opportunity to purchase a Bantam book for only 50¢. Here's how:

By ordering any five books at the regular price per order, you can also choose any other single book listed (up to a $5.95 value) for only 50¢. Some restrictions do apply, so for further details send for Bantam's catalog of titles today.

Just send us your name and address and we'll send you Bantam Book's SHOP AT HOME CATALOG!